PRAISE FOR DAVID HAYNES AND
RIGHT BY MY SIDE

"One of the best young voices in American literature."
—*Minneapolis Star Tribune*

"Haynes offers engaging characters who tackle
fundamental issues such as love, family, and
benevolence."—*Publishers Weekly*

"[Haynes is] a prose writer of the first order—his
firm, biting sentences snap you awake and justify your
attention. . . . Marshall Finney is good company. . . . One of
the most winningly cynical attitudes this side of
Holden Caulfield."—*Hungry Mind Review*

"Haynes's artful fiction should appeal to a wide audience."
—*Kirkus Reviews*

Right by My Side

A NOVEL BY
DAVID HAYNES

Delta
Trade Paperbacks

A Delta Book
Published by
Dell Publishing
a division of
Bantam Doubleday Dell Publishing Group, Inc.
1540 Broadway
New York, New York 10036

ISBN: 0-385-31889-8

Reprinted by arrangement with New Rivers Press

Manufactured in the United States of America
Published simultaneously in Canada

February 1998

10 9 8 7 6 5 4 3 2

BVG

For my family,
who have always been by mine.

ACKNOWLEDGEMENTS

THE AUTHOR THANKS the following for their assistance in the creation of this book: Mary P. Clemons, Leonard Lang, Laura Littleford, Cindy Filipek Johnson, Daniel T. Max, Alice Martell, Karen Hering, Paul J. Hintz, Bill Truesdale, Katie Maehr, and David Cline.

Special thanks to the Cummington Community of the Arts, where most of this novel was written, and to the Ragdale Foundation and the Virginia Center for the Creative Arts, which have provided nurturing environments for my work to grow.

Also to my friends and family—this is what you get for putting up with me. (Extra special thanks to Brian and Jim who water the plants when I'm gone.)

Chapter One appeared in a slightly different form in *Other Voices*.

New Rivers Press wishes to extend its heartfelt thanks, in memoriam, to Garth Tate and the Dayton Hudson Foundation.

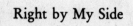

Right by My Side

I

I'M A VERY dangerous boy. I've been known to say almost anything.

Sam and Rose—two people who are supposed to be my parents—have washed out my so-called fresh mouth with soap more than once, but not since I turned fifteen and turned into an overgrown moose. Just maybe it was my big mouth got us into this mess. I don't think anyone knows or cares. It's been more than a year since all this started. Here we are: right back where we began. Same old Sam and Rose and Marshall. Probably forever and ever and ever.

*

That February day was a bad day from the get go.

Such as:

I walk into this class. World Literature for Sophomore Redneck Pinheads, I think they called it. Miss O'Hare is having Black Studies week in 1986 for the first time in her life, and if she flashed her nasty yellow teeth at me one more time, anyway, I'd have knocked them down her throat. We read—get this—excerpts from *Tom Sawyer*. Aunt Polly sends the nigra Jim to fetch Huck and Becky and Tom for victuals.

Pinheads. Each and every one.

"I thought today," says O'Hare, "that we would have a discussion about Black slang. It has made such an important contribution to our language. Let's brainstorm a list of expressions which I'll record on the board. Shall we? Who will begin?"

I'm sitting there wth sixteen or seventeen of them. Pink cheeked and cheery, looking at each other out of the sides of their eyes. O'Hare, scanning for a sucker, catches my eye, hopefully. I drop out my bottom lip about four inches and look at her as if she's asked me to explain nuclear fission. I want to drool, but that would be a little too much.

Finally, she is saved by sophomore class president Connie Jo Hartberger. "I have heard a few times some of them say the word *crucial*. As a slang word, I mean."

"Very good, Connie Jo," says Ohairy, wiping the sweat from her upper lip. She records it on the top of the list.

Connie Jo beams proudly. Her father is a vice president at General Dynamics. He bought her a Honda because she got a B+ in advanced algebra. She told me how "neat" she thought it was that there were now black kids at her school.

"Who can tell us?" Miss O'Hare pushes on, "Does any one here know what *crucial* means? How is it used?"

She knows better than to call on me. I'd tell her it would be crucial if someone peeled the Youth for Reagan bumper sticker from Connie Jo's Civic and pasted it over her fat butt. That would also be "neat."

The slang lesson limps along. On the board she scrawls a list of ten or so worn out and ancient words: *bad, cool, far out*. Ohairy is beet-faced and stammering.

Buzz Simpkins, from whose daddy's dealership Connie Jo got her Honda, raises his hand up by his thick linebacker neck. Buzz's class election commercial featured farting and belching, and a rousing version of "We Are the World." It was a big hit. He is our sophomore class secretary/treasurer. Quick, Buzz: How many pennies in a dollar?

Miss O'Hare calls on him tentatively.

"I know one," he simpers, "but I don't know that I ought to say it. Haw haw haw."

"Use your discretion," teacher encourages. Not even she will look at him.

The pinheads wait on the edge of their chairs. Miss O'Hare poses, chalk at the ready.

"Here goes nothing." Buzz clears his throat. "Your mama. Haw haw haw."

The chalk freezes on the Y, trembling. No one moves. Todd, my red-headed friend who sits behind me, swallows loudly, just as if he knows what to expect.

He does.

The dozens, huh? I stand up. "How about this. Your mammy, your pappy, your whole goddamn family and everyone you know." I get my stuff and walk. I bet they all pissed their pants, too. Everyone of them.

*

So I overreacted. Put up with what I put up with and you'd have an edge on you, too.

*

Such as:

After all of that, after the wise-ass A.P. Mr. Shannon gives me a letter "trusting you'll show your parents," lets me off with a warning "this time, considering the situation," after I have Todd and our other lame-brained friend Artie forge a suitable ass-kissy response to it, which I then have to edit because Todd has such a foul mouth and because Artie is so illiterate, (Artie: "You won't be having no more trouble with our son"; Todd: "We beat Marshall's ass real good when we got your note"), after we ride the school bus across west Saint Louis County, Missouri's finest real estate, through rolling fields, and by green-lawned country clubs, past the landfill to the top of Washington Park, after all of that:

I come through the front door—which is of course wide open even though it is all hours of the day—and there's ma and she says to me, "Do me a favor and fill this up."

No "How are you?" No "Have a good day?" No nothing.

She's got this glass held out to me and there she sits: one hand with the glass, the other stretched before her, arm's length, holding a novel. She is on the green-plaid couch, sitting at an impossible angle with her legs curled to the side like an S. The television set is on—daytime PBS, she watches. Shows about pets and about acrylic painting; it is background noise only. Her eyes never leave the novels. Mysteries with such names as *I Walk the Night,* and *The Bracelets of Bangkok.* She's got on a new dress today. White and frilly, and she's shod with clunky-heeled shoes. Her sharp shiny fingernails are the color of strawberries to match the shoes.

The dress ought to have been a clue to what was up, but I wasn't as good at this stuff then as I am now.

She jiggles the ice in the glass. I walk right by, grinding my Nikes into her yellow, short-shag, stall-to-stall carpeting. I throw my notebooks in my room. Then I go change the TV – to the Flintstones.

She jiggles the glass again. Like a chump I give in and get her some more Kool-Aid. Grape. There is a loud snap as I slam it down on the glass-topped coffee table, right on the crack where Daddy fell into it last New Year's Eve. Another three inches: not a bad addition if I don't say so myself. She ignores the crack and scratches my arm by way of thanks.

"What's for dinner?" I want to know.

"What are you fixing?" she answers.

"Shoot," I say, and go get a snack. I munch some plain Cheerios, catching the little dried circles on my eye teeth and crushing them with my tongue. I lie down and nap in front of the set. Wilma and Barney and Fred wander in and out of my dreams. Dino the dinosaur, on the 26-inch set, is the size of a full-grown cat. Ma stays there posed with the mystery.

When Gilligan comes on, "Look at this," I say to her, "Daddy'll be here soon."

"All right, for Christsake," she seethes. She goes to the kitchen and starts banging stuff around. God knows what dinner will be. Canned corned beef with leftover eggs. Nacho cheeseburger helper. This is a woman who named me after a department store. Marshall Field Finney. Connie Jo Hartberger throws away garbage in bags with my name on them.

From the floor by the TV I can see the top part of her in there wandering aimlessly. "How was school today?" she asks in the pass-through-bar window. Moms are always on that. On with those questions. Dip, dip, dip.

"Fine. Artie and Todd and I poured brown dye in the swimming pool and set the football bleachers on fire."

"That's nice," she says. That's how much she really cares. "Have you by any chance seen anywhere my little portable radio?"

"I'm trying to watch TV," I answer.

Something crashes purposely in the sink. I sit up and meet her eyes. The red claws are spread and taut on the counter, and pointed in my direction. She glares at me, but I don't look away. Her eyes are red, too. I wonder how much sleep she's been getting. Neither of us blinks.

Just then, in walks Daddy. "Still in front of that set, I see. You'll rot your mind."

I don't say a word. Sam wears his striped bibs that make him tall and lean, except he looks around the middle as though he's swallowed a whole salami. All swelled up like a snake that just ate.

"Evening, Sam," she says.

"Rose." He drops on the couch and picks up the paper. Dust rises like steam from his overalls.

"You want a beer, Daddy?" I ask, waving away the cloud. She is already passing a Budweiser through for him.

He closes one giant paw around the can. His fingers meet easily, squeezing out the first swallow and slightly crushing the can. The clay and soot from his fingers mix with the sweat on the can forming rivers of mud.

"Good day today, Sam?" she asks.

"Fine, Rose." he answers.

Sam. Rose. Not Big Sam, or Rosie, or honey or sweetie. Clue #2, that ought to have been. Unfortunately at the time I am caught up in the Hillbillies. Mr. Drysdale is trying to convince the Clampetts that the climate in southern California is getting colder by turning the air conditioning in the Beverly Hills mansion down as far as it will go. Life was in black and white back then. In real life Sam "tsk, tsks" at the headlines, Rose bangs away in the kitchen, and I am too stupid to figure out what's up.

"If you're going to eat this stuff, best get it now."

5:15. One thing for her—she's always on time.

She's set on the table two plastic plates and two glasses of green liquid. And a casserole.

Daddy scoops up a big helping and starts shoveling it in.

I take a little and test it. Tuna and macaroni. That was it. No sauce. No spice. Nothing.

"You expect me to eat this slop?" I say. I turn the plate over on the table and cross my arms.

"Look here, Sam." she says. "You better tell this little nigger of yours something."

"Ug," Sam gurgles. His mouth is full of the crap.

"Clean it up," she says.

I don't move. Then I get up and open the refrigerator door.

She kicks it closed, hard, with her foot, leaving a half-moon-shaped indentation near the center. "There's your dinner," she says, pointing to the mess.

Big Sam's like he's turned to stone. I go get the Cheerios out of the cupboard again.

"Give me that," she says. She grabs the other side of the box. I pull. The cardboard rips. Cheerios fly and land everywhere: dots, pyramids, and rings all over her sticky linoleum floor. It looks like a code.

"Goddamn you to hell," she says, and bursts into a shaking fit of tears.

I go to my room and slam the door and look at the ceiling a while. I do that a lot. Look at the ceiling. From my bed. It is white and gravelly. If you stare long enough you can see things in it.

I'm not staring long this time. After all: I live here too.

I come out and park in front of the set. Lucy and Ricky. I'll grab some grub when the coast's clear. Sam and Rose are really into it now—a continuation of last night and the last month and forever. I've probably missed the best parts.

"It's those filthy hoodlums he runs with," she's saying. "Thieves and delinquents. Urchins."

A lot she knows. Artie writes thank you notes for the thank you notes he gets, and Todd is afraid of almost everything. Loud noises, shadows, even some common vegetables. What's more, he is even white.

Ma goes right on . . .

". . . and here I am stuck in a crackerbox house with a . . . trash man and a loud mouth child. I could have been something."

"Rose, please," sighs Sam.

"Don't touch me," she sobs. And she starts stomping back and forth from the kitchen to her bedroom, to the toilet, to the closet. Stomp, stomp, stomp.

"My mother tried to warn me," she hollers.

That old line, I think to myself. Sam's at the table with his head in his big hands. Sick from the food, no doubt.

Ma stops behind me after a while and I can feel her eyes on me. I turn slowly. Her face is pale beige and her much too red cheeks are streaked with tears. The blue raincoat drapes over her arm and a purse hangs from her shoulder—a little girl's purse on a long metal chain. Just then I know she is really going.

"I can't anymore," she says to me. "I'm sorry."

I turn back to the TV. "Good riddance," I mumble.

Back in the kitchen she and Sam whisper. "No!" he shouts. He comes and stands in front of the door by which she has placed one packed bag. "No, I won't let you." He blocks the door.

"Get out of my way," she says.

I watch the action in the round mirror just above the set. Sam and Rose — framed in smoky-engraved curlicues and butterflies. They aren't looking at each other. Daddy's closed up like a little boy hiding something behind him in a corner. He's looking around like he doesn't know where to look. Our reflected eyes meet.

Come on Sam: use those big hands. Show her who's the boss round here.

"Please." she says. "Don't make this worse. Sam."

Just as he moves to step out of her way she swings the suitcase back to hit him with it. The Samsonite catches him in the groin and he topples over.

And she is gone.

He lies there a long time. So, finally I go over to him.

"Are you all right?" I ask. "Want another beer?"

"Rose," he whines. "My sweet Rosie."

I tell him to get up.

2

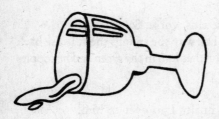 As I THINK about it I probably don't want to be telling all this. If I could get it all into my head at once, I'd probably say "I'm not putting this story out for the whole world to see. It's too personal," and me, I'm not the sort to spread my personal business up and down the street. If folks want to get their jollies, let em do it someplace else. But, what the hell, I was just a dumb kid then, anyway, and I know now that real life is not always pretty to look at. You got to face that. You got to be honest. Real life is also one of those "he goes" and then "she goes" deals. You start telling, and once you get going like that, you can't stop. Before you know it, you come to the end, and, if you're lucky, you've figured something out. But even though I already know how this whole story goes, I'm gonna run it by again to see what I come up with this time. I might know some different stuff now that I didn't know back then. Little things. About him and her. And me.

Pay attention. The goal of these deals, at least as I figure it, is to see if you can make it come out so you look real good on the last page.

I'll pick up the story early next morning and try to remember to get in all the good parts.

*

All night long I hear Big Sam pacing the floor, opening doors, checking dresser drawers.

As if he expected her to pop up jack-in-the-box style and say "gotcha" at any time. Like this was some big joke or something.

He's playing cat and mouse with me, too, so as we don't have to run into each other. I catch him peeking out to make sure the coast is clear at 2:30, a time when almost every night Sam and I run into each other at the bathroom. That's when the famous Finney bladder fills. Every night like clockwork. I'm right on schedule, and I hear him in there bouncing back on his bed, trying to sneak, pretending like this ain't our usual time to pee. Where's my pat on the head? I always get a pat on the head. I think it's leftover from when I was a baby and old what's-her-name claimed I'd wet her mattresses every night. She's a lie, among other things. After I close my door, I hear Sam open his. Like I was going to demand answers, give him the fifth degree in the middle of the night.

You got any answers, Big Sam? You know what's the story here? Naw, you ain't got no answers.

He's laying in there listening for that key in the lock. Listening for the pitter-patter of little feet in big high heels. Go to sleep, old man. What this is, is one of those head game deals. You and me, we're supposed to be having a big fit, right about now. We are supposed to call the police and the sheriff — we're supposed to call out the National Guard. We are supposed to be lying here waiting.

Do you see me in here worrying? Hell, no. Don't give it another thought. After all: how far could she get? She's a mom. Mom's be getting on your nerves — always doing some stuff like this. She's just down at Lucille's or up at Miss Ida's. She'll be sitting there on the couch tomorrow just like every other day — reading that trash, doing her nails, trying to get into my personal business. She'll cook up another batch of slop and things'll be right back to normal.

Give yourself a break, big guy. Go to sleep.

*

Next thing I know, what almost never happens here happens: the alarm clock buzzes. Loud. Usually Mrs. Big Sam is carrying-on, yelling or threatening you to get up with buckets of cold water — that being her version of a very funny joke at six-thirty in the morning. It is seven. Sam is already gone, pickup truck and all. The Cheerios are where they were last night: scattered on the floor. The pile of slop still hides beneath its melmac shelter. Perhaps it has grown green slime and legs and will ooze off the table and fill the whole house by lunch time. The Casserole that ate Washington Park. When Ma comes back expecting a warm welcome . . . well, it won't be a pretty sight.

Sam hasn't eaten. No coffee made, no burned black skillets in the sink. Sam's version of cooking: cook it and keep cooking it until you're sure it's good and dead.

Living here is sort of like living with a deranged Uncle Ben and Aunt Jemima.

I guess he'll have sense enough to feed himself someplace. I hope so.

*

The bus stops for Eisenhower High at 7:30. The boys and me catch it up by Miss Ida's store.

Miss Ida's store is to the right, up the hill on Dorset, on the morning side of the hollow. Sam says that long ago Miss Ida's daddy, L. W., ran moonshine out of a back-country roadhouse right there — last stop before Kansas City. He says it was a regular Dodge City sort of deal, with cheap women and cheap booze, and on a Saturday night he says they'd haul many a chopped up nigger and a few white folks out of there, too. According to Sam, one time his daddy and L. W. was holed-up in the back room, holding off some bootleggers with a couple of old shotguns. Same guns they used to hunt squirrels with. He says you can still see the bullet holes on the side of the store. Who knows what to believe of his old timey stories. I don't see any bullet holes. Sam is always talking some mess.

Miss Ida's store is on the main drag now: Colerain Road, and right out front the buses come and go for Eisenhower and for just about everywhere else in Saint Louis County, as well.

My favorite thing about Miss Ida's store is the way it smells. No other place I know smells just like it: strange and exotic smells — cinnamon, garlic and cheese, old burlap sacks which maybe hold coffee or nuts. There is a pickle barrel, and if you want, Miss Ida will drill a tunnel in a fat sour one and fill it with a peppermint stick. Nothing better with a grape Nehi soda on a hot July day. That's the truth.

The place is a mess, though. Boxes block the doors, and a fine layer of dust covers a bunch of old-fashioned cans of B'rer Rabbit Molasses. I dare anybody to eat any of that molasses, and who knows what other nasty old stuff is laying around up here. Artie's not much help keeping it together. Once, Miss Ida asked him to alphabetize the canned goods for her. She's still looking for the cream-style corn.

Each morning we meet Artie here for school, Todd and I do. Artie comes down all sleepy-eyed from the apartment over the store, except for when he stays down the hollow with Miss Ida's daughter, Betty Lou. People say Miss Ida is too old to have a teenage boy messin about, but she always acts glad to see him in the morning. Us too. She never sends us on our way without something sweet.

"Morning Mr. Marshall," she says. "You out bright and early. You even ahead of Baby Boy." Baby Boy: that is her pet name for Artie. He must have spent the night down at Betty Lou's. She puts a cold Coke on the counter just for me.

"Thanks." I say, taking a long pull. "My daddy been in?"

"Haven't seen Big Sam since yesterday noon," Miss Ida says. "You need something? I'll get him a message later." She pauses in that sentence just long enough for me to wonder if she knows anything.

"No, ma'am." Best not air the family dirty laundry anywhere in the hollow. Everyone in Washington Park knows everything about everyone else. And the best stories — who's doing it with who, who got shot because of it — cross Miss Ida's counter faster than change for a dollar.

Ida's doing the crossword from the *Post Dispatch*. It is usually quiet here in the morning. Her big rush times are at lunch, or in the evening when folks stop in for a cold six pack of Busch or a can of nutmeg. You wouldn't stop here at all unless you knew about it. The weathered boards outside are faded to gray from green, and the 7-Up signs are rusted to pink. Nothing — not the gravel lot, not the ragged canvas awnings — testifies to what or who might be inside. Those other folks drive right on by to the 7-Eleven, and let 'em, anyway. Everyone in the hollow shops Miss Ida. What else would you do?

Artie comes in at 7:25 with Todd on his heels just like some Irish setter. Todd would never come in here without one of us. And not that anyone would notice either: when you hang around black folks long enough, people just assume you're one of us — even if you do have red hair and blue eyes. Not coming in, well that's just how Todd is: shy and afraid, always waiting for someone to tell him what he's done wrong. He nods at me where I wait over by the pickle barrel. He comes over to join me.

"You didn't tell your dad about yesterday at school, did you?" Todd asks me.

I tell him no.

"I wouldn't want mine to find out," he says. "My ass would be a goner. What do you think yours will do?"

"I've got everything under control," I whisper. I shush him by nodding in the direction of the usual morning spectacle developing across the room.

Miss Ida, after getting her standard morning kiss and hug, is tugging at Artie's seams and collars, making him turn around for the full inspection. This goes on every damn morning. When she's done, she holds him at arm's length, admiring her work.

"Don't you look fine," she gushes. "Come on and give Mama one more kiss before that bus gets here."

Artie blushes, warming his deep tan skin almost the way hot water might. His hair is shaved close to the scalp on the sides, and picked up on the top. Mr. High Fashion is the first person I actually know to ever get that box cut. It naturally suits the shape of his boxy skull, and even his hair seems to color when he blushes. I make a kissy face so Miss Ida can't see me, but it doesn't have any effect. As much as I tease, the fact is, he likes it . . . likes giving Mama a big kiss every morning, even in front of the boys. Maybe if Miss Ida was mine I'd like it too. Still, you have to wonder about folks who carry-on like this. There's something soft about Artie, something mushy and weak. I say you got to be strong. Hard and strong so they can't get you. Take Todd, for instance. He may be skittery and even thin-skinned, but he wouldn't cry even if you stuck toothpicks under his fingernails. My kind of man.

As for me, I'm rather ornery, even if I do say so myself.

*

Eisenhower High School is nothing and nowhere. From the road it is another unfortunate pile of suburban bricks—it could be the telephone company or sewage treatment plant—and every day is the same there, and nothing of consequence ever goes on. But just tell that to the Pinheads inside. For them every day might be the first day of the Royal American Shows. You could cut the high spirits here with a dull butter knife.

Pinheads:

They make a person want to stop every other one of em up in here and ask if they have a license to be as stupid as they act. These people are always laughing—har har har. As if white folks were in on some big private joke. But when you listen to them it's either what funny thing happened to somebody's new car or else some warmed-over line from "Saturday Night Live." For a while there it was "You look mahvelous. You look mahvelous." Till you wanted to puke. It wasn't even that funny in the first place. They go around saying those stale lines like they made them up themselves, and then they laugh like it was the first time they'd heard them. Har, har, har.

"Lighten up, Finney," they say: you know how they call everybody by the last name, and I get turned in to Mr. Shannon, the A.P., for being sullen. Sullen means white folks' stale jokes don't strike you as funny.

"Are you unhappy, Marshall?" Shannon asks. "We want ya'll to be happy here."

Well, the first thing you white folks need to do is get the fuck out of my face.

Of course I don't say that.

It takes all my energy most days to keep from turning into a Pinhead myself.

It is 1:00. The air in Redneck World Literature is charged. Buzz Simpkins broods, his thick neck sunk deep into his shoulders. Connie Jo looks hurt and disappointed, as though she's been slapped by her baby brother. She looks like one of those rich women who come around Washington Park at Christmas and can't figure out why folks don't want their used clothes.

The air is supercharged. The smallest spark could set it off and annihilate a large part of Saint Louis County. Neighboring communities would be buried in a fallout of greasy pink flesh.

Miss O'Hare, cautious if anything, runs her class as if it were a dynamite truck crossing the Alps. No detail is beyond her control. We are greeted at the door with a page of questions, texts placed on our desks already opened to Martin Luther King's "Letter from Birmingham Jail." O'Hare's hair is drawn tightly behind her head in a ponytail.

She's in one of her moods. For almost nothing she'd pop that rubber band off her hair and blast someone in the face with it.

"Today you will read Dr. King's essay, after which I expect you to complete the handout. When you are finished you are to begin reading the novel excerpt from *Native Son*. The glossary in the back of your text will help you with the essay."

In other words: come near this desk and die.

"Be prepared to discuss this material and be quizzed on it. Tomorrow. Are there any questions?"

Yes. Who do you think you are, up there like that, walking back and forth, having the nerve to call yourself a teacher? Just who do you think you are? Of course I don't ask it at this time.

O'Hare removes her brown-framed glasses and sets them on the desk in front of her. No contact lenses today. Her blue cardigan sweater has the effect of a policeman's uniform. She taps her ruler in her hand as if it were a nightstick, all the while scanning back and forth inviting any and all trouble with a stack of detention slips, date and crime already filled in. Everyone watches her out of the top of their eyes, heads bent over in nervous concentration. We've been here before.

One day last fall Buzz decided it might be fun if we all stared at the same spot on the wall behind her. And so we did. When O'Hare walked in front of a person, he or she would sort of lean to the side as if to see around her. O'Hare even looked back there a few times herself before she caught on.

"What are you looking at?" she said coldly. "Mr. Simpson? Mr. Finney?" She went down the roll asking each one.

Of course, no one responded. We all just sort of hung our heads.

"Perhaps you need a reminder of who's in charge of this class and why I'm here," she said.

On a day like today there was little doubt about that.

Ohairy stops behind my desk during one of her regular rounds. "I'd like to see you after class," she says. "And watch out for double negatives." She makes a big red slash under what I consider a perfectly good English sentence.

I'd been called out.

So there I stand in front of her desk, books caught behind my back, feet shoulder length apart.

"Yes, ma'am," I say.

Miss O'Hare stands up on her side of the desk; I have to raise my eyes slightly to meet hers.

She addresses me by looking me right in the eye. "First of all, a little technical matter: I've noticed on your papers this tendency to use *like* as a conjunction."

I give her a retarded face. The one Artie uses, except with him sometimes I don't think he means to be doing it.

"I'll give you an example. Listen to this – from one of your papers: 'In those days people took care of each other like family was the most important thing in the world.' Not good." She shakes her head and makes a prune face. "People don't even bother to hear your ideas unless they are in good standard English. It's worth your time to master it.

"Now, I know that people talk that way, but just work on it, okay? The other thing is: about the other day." This time she makes a face as if she thought we'd shared some stupid experience that neither of us could believe.

"Yesterday's slang lesson got . . . ridiculous, out of my control. I thought I knew what I was doing but . . . It won't happen again. These black history lessons aren't for my benefit, and I know you've already had most of this stuff, right?"

I give her my blank look.

"Wonderful!" she gushes.

What some mistake for smarts – my open mouth, my bulgy eyes – is often only mindless drooling.

"What really bothers me is: I tried to give you an opportunity to show what you know and you passed it up."

"Huh?" I say.

Real mature response, huh?

"It's the same as the commercial says – a mind is a terrible thing to waste. I've had my eye on you. I've been looking for someone like you for a long time. When I see someone with a spark, I'm willing to stick my neck out. If you don't want me to do it – fine. Just don't make me look foolish. Clear?"

I nod. She hands me a pass to the next class.

*

So: How am I supposed to react to her little pep talk? Was that an apology? An explanation? Am I supposed to feel humiliated? Scolded?

What about Buzz? The other Pinheads? Did they get off with just a day of the famous Ohairy cold shoulder?

Artie and Todd and I are clustered near the back of the bus as usual. Old habits die hard. In junior high school you could talk dirty if you sat in the back. We did. Todd would practice stringing together as long a list of smutty words as possible. His record was ten different words in the same sentence. Just imagine. You'll have to, cause not even me is about to put some of those words on paper. These days cursing isn't even fun, and the back seats are just another place to sit.

"I'd tell my mom is what I'd do. I wouldn't let no teacher talk to me that way." Artie says. He adjusts the neck to his Benetton sweater. He is quite the dude: Miss Ida has him everyday looking like he just stepped out of the Saks Fifth Avenue ad or something. He sticks out like a black cat in a snow storm. Not that he dresses better or worse than the Pinheads. It's just so . . . perfect: creased trousers, tie bars, collar stays. Like he was somebody's daddy or something.

Todd calls Artie a "fucking mama's boy" and then says to me, "I'd leave well enough alone. You got off pretty easy."

Todd speaks mostly in whispers. He is quiet and to the point, though like everybody else, he is sometimes full of a lot of crap that you don't really want to listen to.

Like now.

I tell him so. I say, "I didn't do anything. So what was there to let me off easy for? Ohairy's not being fair."

"You had another fuckin tantrum is what for," Todd says. "All your life, when things get rough, you lose your temper and then you holler like a girl 'It's not fair, it's not fair.' Like in second grade when you told . . ."

"You and your ancient history can kiss my ass." I say.

"I believe back then it was kiss my black ass, and you said it to that sweet old Miss Adkins. She had to retire after you."

"She was a hundred and six years old. And we're talking about fairness. Did Ohairy call out Buzz? No. Only the black kid. That's what I call unfair."

"Jesus Christ, Marshall. You never learn. If the teacher yells — it's unfair, if the bus is late — it's unfair. Your mom burns dinner . . ."

"My mom ran away from home last night."

Nobody says anything for a minute. They look to see if I'm serious.

16

Artie looks away embarrassed. I raise my hand in a way to indicate that it's okay.

That's how I worked it in. That's how I got it out.

Todd continues quietly, "Well, anyway, you never learn. If Artie and I . . ."

"Two chickenshits, might I add."

". . . weren't here to keep you in line . . . Forget it." Todd looks away.

I make some clucking noises.

Todd's gone back to staring out the window. Todd is usually staring out the bus window. You have to wonder what it is he sees out there. He's always been that way. Always at the window. The cold air turns his freckled cheeks redder and a draft teases at his tangled shoulder-length hair. No one at Eisenhower except for Todd has hair this long. That combined with the fact he runs with Artie and me . . . well he might as well be as black as coal.

Todd could never finish an argument either.

"Thanks for nothing," I say. I make some more clucking noises.

Artie fixes a cuff as he waves me off with his watch hand. I see the sparkle of the diamond that is where the twelve should be. Todd closes his eyes behind his wire-rimmed glasses. He leans back and gives me the finger.

I love these guys, but sometimes they are just a couple of wimps.

*

Opening the door I understand at once what must be done. First, of course, turn on the TV. The amplified tinny voice of the Flintstones makes everything seem normal. I could turn on MTV, but even though I've seen all of these episodes before — where Pebbles is born, where Gilligan finds the TransPacific telephone cable which has washed up in a hurricane — reruns are just what you need sometimes.

In the kitchen I sweep the Cheerios into a pile and then dump them into the garbage disposal. A gray-beige fountain spouts up until I remember to turn on the water.

On a roll, I scrape the tuna-noodle slop from the table onto the melmac plate and dump it in there, too. That hurts the most: it's a pride thing. I ought to have let that crap rot on the table till it turned to stone. But that could have been a long time. For spite, I dump the melmac plate into the trash bin. That felt good. Those plates are hundred-year-old hand-me-downs, anyway.

When everything in the kitchen looks somewhat as it ought to — not hard considering what usually passes for housework around here — I go to make dinner. The refrigerator holds only a six pack of Budweiser and some eggs. The cupboards hold nothing but canned slop: Vienna sausages, corned beef hash, chili con carne, tomato soup, mushroom soup, fifteen tins of tuna fish, a miniature can of Contadina tomato paste.

Who could even feed their dog?

I run up the hill to Miss Ida's. The store is full of neighbors. They stop talking when I come in the door. I nod "good evening" — the whole polite boy routine — and duck back to the frozen foods. I don't even think I know some of these folks, and what made them all come to the store tonight anyway. Over her glasses Miss Ida gives me one of those looks you give to sick people. I want to go up there and tell them all to mind their own damn business.

Instead, I reach in and get two Jeno's Pizzas. Large. Pepperoni. I tell Miss Ida to put them on my tab. She wants to know since when have I got myself a tab; she waves me out the door with them anyway. She says "take care" in a way that makes me want to scream.

I run home and dump the pizzas into the oven. They should be ready when Sam comes in. I sit in front of the TV and try to act normal.

When Big Sam comes in I see his face in the mirror. He says nothing. He throws his coat across a chair, and I get up to hang it in the closet.

"Leave it," he says.

So there I'm standing with his coat, looking foolish.

He walks down the short hall and looks in the bedroom. Then in the bathroom. Finally the kitchen, the utility room, out the back windows.

"Do you want a beer?" I ask.

He opens the refrigerator and gets himself a beer. He sits down and puts his feet up on one of the yellow upholstered dinette chairs.

"I made us some pizza," I say. I'm standing on the living room side of the pass-through-bar. I don't know what I'm supposed to do.

"You get to school today?"

"Yes, sir."

"Any calls? Mail?"

"No, sir."

I go in and take the pizza from the oven and then cut them up in triangles like they show on the commercials. I set one pizza on a potholder, get down two plates, and make myself a glass of Kool-Aid.

I sit down across from Sam and try to eat a piece of pizza. I have to put it down. The pizza burns my tongue, and he is staring at me.

Staring and staring, so I look down at the pizza waiting for it to cool. We sit this way for about a century.

*

Sam gets up without touching the pizza. He takes another beer and goes in front of the TV. I try again to eat some of the food. Under each piece of pizza a puddle of yellow grease has congealed like snot. I drink the Kool-Aid and put the pizzas in the fridge for another time. I eat Oreo Chip ice cream directly from the box.

I sit on the plaid couch across from Big Sam who is in his chair. Big Sam's chair is a six position, crushed-velvet, orange, vibrating Wall-away recliner. He sits in position one, straight-backed, staring at the TV, not watching a rerun of the Jeffersons. Sam never sits in position one.

"Well," he says, taking a swig off the beer.

"Well," I say.

He sighs and rubs his big hand through his nappy salt-and-pepper hair. His eyes when he looks at me are liquid and empty.

"It'll be okay," I say.

He looks back at the TV and takes another swig of the beer.

"I can always get dinner," I say.

He makes a noise like a snuffling pig, smiles, though it is really a sneer.

"I can. I just need money for groceries. Miss Ida'll give me a tab . . ."

"This ain't none of her business."

"I didn't say nothing to her. I wouldn't."

I didn't tell him she probably already knew. Everyone else in Washington Park, too.

For a while it is quiet again.

Eventually Sam says, "No matter."

I don't understand, but I keep talking anyway. "We'll be okay. You'll see."

Sam empties the beer can, crushes it, and drops it clanging onto the shattered table top. He stands looming over me a good long while, looking down at me over his nose, his lips, his big belly. He turns and walks from the room, saying, "Boy, you don't know shit."

3

SATURDAY MORNING following Rose's big exit scene, about ten, I'm on my way out the door. The boys and I are taking the bus to Chesterfield Mall. They got some nice stuff out there: movie theaters, a video arcade, a McDonald's. We never run out of things to do.

They also have every kinda store you'd want ever, but we don't do much shopping. Artie already has more matching outfits than Barbie herself. Really. Even his socks match. All Todd ever wears are jeans and a T-shirt. Also this army jacket with the name Dawson sewn over the pockets. Todd's name is Lawrence. I asked once who this Dawson is, but Todd just shrugged his shoulders and asked how in the hell was he supposed to know. Sometimes Todd wears a different color T-shirt. The khaki green jacket goes well with his red hair. Often his clothes look clean. There's something rather homemade about them. You get the idea if you pulled a string he'd unravel.

As for me, I wear whatever I wear. Much closer to Todd's taste in that sense. Rose, bless her heart, collects old and new clothes from garage sales. Always something different and new in the dresser. Sometimes the garage sale stuff is ironed, which means that the white ladies over in the subdivision ironed it before they put it out for sale. Rose doesn't believe in ironing. Says if God meant women to iron she wouldn't have invented permanent press.

Before I leave I take a look around the joint. In our crackerbox house things have moved from cluttered toward filthy in five days flat, but I've gotten the message loud and clear: "Leave it." So I have. The whole house has turned into a garbage pit. The kitchen sink is stacked high with piles of plates, sticky with grape jelly. There are Burger King bags and cups and boxes on every counter. In the bathroom on the floor layer after layer of mildewed towels lie crumpled in the corner. And there are beer cans everywhere. Only in my own room have I been able to keep some control on the clutter, rounding up my clothes and sneaking them to the utility room for a quick wash when Sam's back is turned.

"Leave those damned clothes be, boy," he'd shout if he caught me. I swear, this house will smell of year-old cheese before Sam backs down. Meanwhile let's hope the authorities don't catch wind of us.

No chance of that. After all: Big Sam is the mayor of Washington Park. Well, technically there is no such place as Washington Park, so there really isn't such a thing as a mayor. What Washington Park is, is half-a-hundred prefabbed crackerbox palaces just like this one on three cul-de-sacs (as the more uppity residents call them), four dead ends, and two main streets. Guess what one of the main streets is called? Dr. Martin Luther King Drive. It's about two blocks long. It has potholes. It has a storm sewer outlet. It has a two-way stop. Sometimes I think that Dr. King must be spinning in his grave over all the King Drives everywhere. Our King Drive is a dead end. Really.

Don't look for Washington Park on any map. From Colerain Road you see only overgrown brush, scraggly trees, Miss Ida's store. Way off in the distance you can see the Missouri River and Saint Charles County. We are completely invisible from the fancy stuck-up-the-ass subdivisions of Fox Trails and Greenbriar. Think they don't like it that way? Washington Park is halfway down a hollow, a hollow winding to the flood plain. Only the P.W.T. (poor white trash, Todd's people) live further out on the plain, across the tracks down Dorset—truck farmers and river rats, they are.

Rose says they put the white trash further down the hill because as much as your ordinary garden variety white person hates "us," they hate P.W.T. worse. They're embarrassing, she says. Rose says that P.W.T. never throw anything away because they think their even trashier relatives from Arkansas and Kentucky who come up here by the truckloads might need it. She says that all sorts of shameful stuff goes on down there, stuff a person such as herself does not discuss.

Sam says the P.W.T. are harmless; just hard-working poor folk.

Which is about the same as what Todd would say about them if he were ever to say anything about them at all.

Rose says to be careful around that Todd boy anyway.

Washington Park is also the big landfill, the junkpile on Colerain Road. Sam Finney: proprietor. Clean fill only, please. Ten dollars a truckload. Rotten appliances and rotten roofs, light bulbs, dirt, your old couch. Clean — but enough banana peels to keep the rats happy. Washington Park garbage mostly. Local trash pickup, snow removal, and street maintenance also available.

Trash man, street cleaner: those are Sam's jobs. That makes him the mayor of Washington Park.

Sam reports to some white folks over at the Saint Louis County office — that little brick box on King Drive. Them white folks don't live down here, but they come around now and then. They tell Sam when to plow the street, when to turn on the sprinklers. They check on life up at the dump. They bring Sam a paycheck once or twice a month, and mostly they leave him alone. He does what he sees fit. There's a high redwood fence on the Colerain side of the dump. It stretches along all above Washington Park. Sam says the man prefers not to be reminded. They don't even really know we're down here at all, he says, and he also says that that's fine with him: for the best. So long as they leave us alone and we got a roof over our heads. He'll keep the roads paved and clean, and we'll keep to ourselves. Poor folks, black folks, we've always taken best care of ourselves. We are here, and out there is someplace else entirely. That's what Sam says.

Every once in a while he has to go out and break up some little scuffle, or fuss some kids out of the playground. One time — a Saturday — some older dudes were playing ball down in the park. Well, things developed, and by and by a near riot broke out because somebody fouled somebody or somebody bent the hoop. Rose came in hollering, "Get up! Get up! Got some big trouble down the hill." Sam's laid out on the couch, sound asleep like on every Saturday afternoon. He stumbles up and grabs his shotgun. He runs on down there. Everybody in Washington Park was out watching this mess. Sam gets down there and fires his rifle in the air a couple of times. Everybody freezes. Them boys circle each other a few more times, but they got the message. They went on home.

"Well, that's that," Sam said.

He's the mayor, I guess, and sort of the sheriff, too.

Unfortunately the mayor's been a little under the weather this week. And who rules the roost while the rooster's got the blues?

*

As I said, I'm on my way out the door Saturday morning to meet the boys, when behind me I hear, "Just a minute, there," and I turn around and there's Sam wearing some greasy old overalls over his pajamas.

"I'm just going out for a minute," I say. Sam tosses me a red leather-like address book which I recognize instantly as belonging to Rose.

"Call around and see what you can find out," he says, and then he turns back toward his waist-high-in-clutter-and-filth bedroom.

What's the deal here?

I go to his bedroom door. He is in there rooting around, tossing junk from one pile to the next.

"Sir," I say, idly turning the address book as if I don't know what it is.

"Look," he says, waving hands around, "Start with the relatives. Call everybody in the goddamn book if you have to."

"Aren't people going to suspect something?"

"Not if you use that big head of yours. Get started. Let me know."

Great. All of a sudden I'm a private detective.

I get a brainstorm. I call up Artie. Miss Ida answers, which tells me he's down at Betty's. I hang up without saying anything and call him down there. Betty Lou's raspy-sweet voice answers, so I hang up again. I wait a minute or two, tapping on the receiver with my fingers.

"I don't hear calling out there," Sam says.

I call Artie back.

"Yes, uh, hello. This is your cousin from Saint Louis calling, Marshall Finney."

"My sister don't appreciate you playing on the phone, man."

"Nice speaking to you also. Yes. The reason I'm calling is that something has come up and I'm wondering if you could give me some information."

"Big Sam's standing behind you. You can't talk."

"Yes, ma'am, that is correct."

"I hope this don't mean you can't go to the movies."

I laugh one of those polite telephone laughs that Rose always does.

"This is something to do with your mom running off, right?"

"I'll be sixteen in March."

"We'll spring you. I'll make Betty invite you for lunch. Sam can't say no to Betty. Hang in a few minutes." Artie slams down the phone.

I keep right on. "Yes I was wondering if you'd heard anything from my mother lately."

Pause.

"No she's not exactly missing or anything. She's got that amnesia thing."

Pause.

"Please call us if you hear anything." Pause.

"Thanks. I hope to see you soon, too. Bye."

"Who was that?" Sam wants to know. He's standing right there behind me.

"Cousin Reva," I tell him. I don't have any cousin Reva. "You remember. Rose's cousin Melba's second girl."

The bluff works: Sam don't know half his own relatives. Says all them hens are alike to him.

"Get back to work," he orders. "And lose that amnesia shit."

Swell.

So I start through alphabetically:

MISS ELSIE FAY ANDERSON – the queen of Park Baptist Church which Rose attends, but on Easter Sunday and Founder's Day only.

GREAT AUNT ROSALIE BURTON – Rose's namesake. She has a lot of money and is extremely senile.

MR. CHARLES – Rose's hairdresser.

COUSIN THELMA COLLINS – loves Sam, hates Rose, a spiteful witch, according to Ma.

UNCLE LUTHER DIGGS – looks white, talks white, thinks he's white, depressed, depressing.

Thirty-two calls at least I make. "Oh, dear," a lot of them say. "Finally," is a popular comment with the women relatives.

I call my cousin Sheila.

"Sheila, you seen my mom?"

She just laughs. She is just a few years older than me. Where she gets off being so haughty I'll never know.

"What's so funny?" I want to know.

"Come on, cuz. Give it up. She and big daddy having a little tiff, ain't they?"

"Just tell me if you've seen her."

"Ya'll just chill. You know the poem: leave her alone and she'll come home."

"Thanks for nothing." I hang up on her and continue down the list.

I tell some of them that Rose went to the store and we need to talk to her before she comes home and we were just calling in case she happened to stop by on the way. Some I tell that she went on a cross-country driving trip and we'd heard there was some sort of a big storm in their area and we wanted to know if they'd heard from her. Some I just ask if my mama's there.

No one is fooled: I can tell by how they treat me on the phone. They say things like "we haven't heard *yet*" and "I know how you must be feeling." Things that make my ears burn and my face hot. Behind our backs I know the family gossip network is alive with Sam's name and Rose's name and my name, too. That pisses me off. Like I want my name hooked up in some mess like this. She was so eager to get herself up and out of here, did she take a minute to think about me? Hell no. All she saw was the door, the way out, and Sam and me be damned. And here I am on the phone begging for information. I feel like a fool. Never again.

When the phone rings Sam charges out, hitching up his overalls, the desperation piercing his eyes. He nods for me to pick it up.

"Betty wants to know if I can come for lunch with Artie."

Sam's face falls behind its stony mask. I feel foolish and petty.

"You called everyone?"

I nod, too ashamed to speak.

"That girl. What has she done now?" He shakes his head. "What has she got herself into?" He sees me watching him. He cocks his head to indicate I can go.

"Maybe Betty's heard something," I offer, but from Sam there is no reply.

*

All of the houses in Washington Park are painted cheerful pastels — pink, pale green, baby blue — and the shutters are spotless white, even though they are only plywood fakes, serving no purpose, shutting nothing from nowhere. Betty Lou Warner's house, the one she shares sometimes with Artie, just may be the most cheerful of all. It is painted a bright lavender color and surrounded most of the year by oceans of flowers and blooming bushes. Then, at Christmas, Betty Lou's festival of lights – which includes a life-sized manger scene with a light up baby Jesus – outdoes even the shopping malls; it glows through the night almost until the first tulips pop up in the early spring.

Betty's a fun girl. Just about any afternoon and often on the weekend you find Artie there in the almost purple house at the top of Woodlawn Street, a short hill of a street that dead-ends into an overgrowth of scrub trees. Artie's room is up at Miss Ida's store, but I always look for him here first, because Miss Ida quickly gets sick of his foolishness and sends him packing.

When I come in for lunch Betty is ironing Artie's school shirts, and Artie and Todd are in the kitchen on a sandwich assembly line. A Kool filter dangles from the corner of Betty's mouth. Very thin, Betty wears her hair in a short-cropped Afro, and favors tight-fitting clothes, black or else violet, both of which show up good next to her medium brown skin. You can tell she and Artie are each other's people, though her skin is just that much darker than his. Artie says she is around thirty, though she doesn't seem much older than us. Who knows?

"Marshall," she says as I come in. The cigarette drops an ash on the ironing board and she curses. "So we saved you from the big black bear."

"Get some ice," Artie orders, "the sandwiches are almost done."

"Any luck on the phone?" Betty wants to know.

Artie shrugs in a way to let me know that Betty already knows everything. Which she would anyway since she's almost always home, and Artie tells her absolutely everything, and anything else he can think of as well. That boy and his big mouth.

Betty knows everyone's business anyway. She doesn't work, except occasionally relieving her mother at the store. This house is widely believed to be Miss Ida's, and it sits in such a way so that out its front window you can keep up with everyone in Washington Park. That's how Betty spends most of her time.

I tell Betty that the phone was a bust.

"Poor Rose. She always wanted more." Betty absent-mindedly irons some Barbie doll socks.

"Who? More what?" I demand. "I'm sure you can't be talking about my mother." Even I am surprised by my sudden burst of family loyalty.

"Cool, blood. Remember I be knowin her longer than you. We all come up together, albeit she is just that much older than me." Betty Lou makes this last crack real sassy, as if anyone cared about her age or Rose's either. She puts the ironing away and takes over the lunch serving from us boys. Artie resumes his role as lord of the manor, placing himself at the head of the table – Christ, she even serves him first.

With no encouragement from me, Betty goes on:

"Your mom: they broke the mold when they made that girl. Let me tell you."

And she did, but first she pops open and sets in front of each of us a cold beer. You have to love Betty. Miss Ida, Big Sam, and every P.W.T. in Todd's family would have a stroke if they saw us now, sucking on cool ones. Does Betty care? Hell no. She'd tell them where to stick it and how far up, too.

So, there we sit with our Bud Lights, Betty just going on:

"Rose had what you call aspirations. I bet she couldn't quite say what it was she wanted. Money. Fame. Whatever." Betty is alternating drags on her Kool with bites of the ham and cheese sandwhich.

"You boys got everything you need?" she asks, but she's asking this of Artie, and if he'd asked for a cherry pie, she'd have been up right then baking one.

"She met your daddy – and let me tell you right here and now that this was one fine looking nigger back then – oohwee and with a good living and a house too?"

Here she's talking and I'm wishing she's not. How am I supposed to be hearing this? Are these two strangers she's talking about here? Or characters on that "All My Children" show she watches like it was God's truth? This is Sam and Rose.

Todd who has sat there staring at Betty Lou without saying a word, is completely caught up by her tale. His freckled head is tilted to the side and he's got this look on his face – the look you get when you expect someone's about to tell you a dirty joke. I get the idea maybe that P.W.T don't carry on like this at lunch, though who knows what goes on down there. I only went down there once, and there wasn't too much talking when I was there. Betty Lou's thrilled to have such an interested audience and may never stop. I shoot Artie a nasty look.

"Cissy, do you think I could have some of mom's corn relish?" he says by way of saving me.

Corn relish. Jesus, who eats corn relish. It half works, though, since Betty gets up to serve him. She comes back and keeps on with her story.

"Yes, yes, yes. One fine nigger indeed." She plops a little ice cream dish with a clump of yellow mess in front of each of us. "And, despite whatever else she might have wanted, she set her mind to getting Big Sam Finney. Even with his being five years older and what have you. You know what I'm saying?" Betty Lou smirks at her own question.

I'm sitting across the table from Todd who, sensing I'm just about to go off, shakes his head ever so slightly to distract me. Artie nervously eats all three bowls of corn relish. Betty forges ahead, so wrapped up in her tale is she.

"Now I'm going to tell you something you don't know."

"Please, don't," I say flatly, and under the table I feel Todd kick me. Betty Lou doesn't hear me anyway.

"For many years now Mr. Sam Finney has had to keep that girl's reins pulled in tight. *And,* I know for a fact that at least once she has packed up and been on her way. To God knows where."

"That's a goddamn lie," I say. I know full well it might not be.

"I beg your pardon," says Betty, finally stopped. Her face freezes somewhere between confusion and indignation.

"That's not how you speak to my family, mister." Artie tries to puff out his little chest. Todd whispers that he thinks it's time to leave for the movies. Betty Lou rises behind Artie and pets him as if she were soothing a mad dog. A distracted look comes over her—like a person who'd forgotten why she'd gone to the store or something.

"I'll call around," she says sweetly. "I know some folks Rose knows. Maybe I can find something out for you."

I don't say anything.

Todd—quite unlike himself with politeness and words—smothers Betty with thanks for all her hospitality and guides us to the door.

"Uh, Marshall," Betty says. She says "Marshall" like she's forgotten that was my name.

I glare at her.

"It's just that, you might've seen this coming, no?"

I walk away from her toward the bus stop up by the store.

We sit in a 70mm Dolby space movie which I don't see or hear at all. Todd sits between Artie and me, walks between us, separating us, all in all trying to keep the peace. As usual he's got to be calming the waters, changing the subject. He chats in a funny and sad way about how fat and ugly all the former child actors are, about how they really do grind worms into hamburger meat to extend the protein. Todd is good at this: this smoothing over and distracting. As if he were afraid the worst would happen if he stopped. All the girls from Eisenhower who have a crush on Todd's red hair and gray-blue eyes go out of their way to bump into us at the mall. He whispers "slut" and "cow" behind their backs. Todd doesn't like your run-of-the-mill shopping mall girl. He says they are ignorant and only good for one thing, and for that, he says, with those skags, you would have to worry that afterwards you would get some kind of disease and your thing would fall off.

"Look at those two," he says. It is a couple of fat girls with halters. He makes snuffling noises as they pass.

I cannot focus on his nonsense. Just how was I supposed to "see this coming?" What: are they making Cliff's notes and score cards for family trauma these days?

Sure, Rose rode her high horse, and Sam eased through life, every day the same as the day before. I could have been their toaster or any other useless kitchen appliance — that's how much I mattered. All families are like this, and the truth is: so what? A bored and unhappy woman goes her way and does her own thing. Sam will survive eventually, and my life will get better or it won't. These things just happen.

Up on the screen silver ships dodge and duck missiles, and a whole world explodes. I don't even know how they make that happen, yet, somehow I should have "seen this coming." I lean over to tell Artie that his sister is full of shit, but Todd pins me to my chair.

I interrupt the silence on the bus ride home.

"I really hope she never comes back," I say.

Todd says please not to talk about this anymore. I tell him I want to. To say it now. Say it so it won't need to be said ever again.

"What sort of person does something like this? Runs off. Leaves her family. I mean, everyone thinks their parents are weird, but this is too much. It's mean. Selfish and mean."

"I don't think you believe that," says Artie. As if he'd know what anyone believed. Artie: always saying what he thinks he ought to.

I tell him it's so. "I'm through with her. If this is her attitude, fine. She can go on about her business. Whatever that is. Good luck to her."

"What about your dad?" Todd asks. "There's more people involved in this than you."

"Don't you worry about my dad. I'll take care of him."

*

Big Sam is waiting for me in his orange chair.

"Your Aunt Lucille called."

Oops. Before I can b.s. as to how calling her slipped my mind, how I'd decided not to call, how I didn't get an answer, Sam says:

"I guess the old bitch caught wind on the family grapevine that we were looking for your mama."

Lucille is Rose's mother's sister. She could smell family trouble across the continental divide, and the Central West End is a lot closer than that. There's been bad blood between her and Sam ever since she floor-showed at the big wedding. I understand that names such as "heathen" and "dried up old heifer" were exchanged, and that Rose herself fainted dead away — organdy, orange blossoms, and all.

"Let's get our stories straight," Sam says. "I told her you were upset and confused and that everything is fine."

"Sure thing," I say, nodding, sealing the pact.

"You cover the phone. You know when to come get me."

"Yes, sir." More nodding.

He calls me a good boy and rubs me on the head before ushering a six pack to his room. I won't see him again today.

*

About eleven the phone rings. I turn from Johnny Carson, and there Sam is. His eyes are bleary red and he is halfway into a rumpled pair of pajamas. He nods at the phone. I just look at it. It rings some more; Sam nods again.

"Hello," I say.

"Marshall. Is that you, Marshall?"

Lying with my eyes, I shake my head at Big Sam. I say hello again. "Please put your daddy on the phone. Please."

"No, I think you have the wrong number."

Big Sam crumples his fists in disappointment.

"Marshall." Rose's voice sounds distant and vague.

"That's quite all right," I say, and I hang up. I put a hand on Big Sam's shoulder and walk him to bed. The phone rings again.

"Go on to bed. I'm sure it's that same wrong number. Let it ring. She'll give up sooner or later."

4

So THIS is what I do next.

I figure what Sam doesn't miss won't hurt him.

I start cleaning house. Spring cleaning, but I do it from the bottom of the pile up. Quite the trick. And I do it fast and on the sly, in the morning after Sam leaves, and just after school before he comes in from the landfill.

I turn on MTV. Loud. I play it through the stereo. You don't need the pictures, anyway, once you've seen them. They get stuck in your head.

I go fishing around in these stacks of towels, pulling out one or several to wash. What you do when you pull off the bottom is, fluff up the top of the pile so it looks like nothing much has changed. The music blasts, the house rocks.

Here are some things I learned:

TEN BEER CANS look like twenty when they are arranged just so.

YOU CAN'T TELL dirty overalls from clean ones when they're thrown back on the floor. Well, maybe from the smell you can.

That's how I fool Big Sam and that's how days turned into weeks. Sam becomes more of a zombie, and days on end go by when he doesn't say more to me than "ug" or "pass the salt."

He stops the "leave it be," and after a time I make the house livable once more. So bold am I, I begin to make the place the way I'd like it.

Such as:

Why is it better that all the towels match anyway? I put them out in patterns to suit my fancy—stripes with flowers, black with pink. Hell, poor people would be happy just to have clean ones. Also, I take all of those wimpy face-sized towels on which you can't hardly even get a good nose wipe and stack them way the hell in the back of the closet where they're out of the way for good. Rose bought those rags because she saw them in *Better Homes and Gardens*. If they showed silk toilet paper, we'd be sittin pretty.

Further:

If I want my socks and underwear in the same drawer, well, dammit, that's the way it's going to be. And I lay my socks side by side like nature intended. Not in those crappy little balls that Rose makes which cause the top of one sock to lose all its elastic and ride on your ankle like an old tire. Where do women learn that crap anyway?

Miss Ida bags up dinner groceries for Big Sam almost daily but for some reason he doesn't want me handling them. I make my wishes known when I stop by the store after school and say things like "that Polish sausage sure looks nice" and "I've been craving chicken nuggets lately." Like magic, whatever I want shows up in Sam's dinner bag.

Sam sets the bag on the table and even starts to cook sometimes, but I figure either he doesn't quite know how to cook or else it's just too damn discouraging. Before long he's back sitting with a Bud listening to Dan Rather drawl on about the world situation or some such thing. I finish up myself, stirring and frying. One thing about being the only living heir to the Finney estate: learn to cook young or starve for sure.

I try for a while setting a nice table, but figure, what the hell—especially since sometimes Sam eats what I cook, and sometimes he just picks at it. So, I serve myself a big helping of whatever and sit right in front of the TV and eat it up. By and by here's Sam doing the same thing. We've got ourselves a regular bachelor pad going. Sometimes we watch the news. Sometimes we watch videos. Sometimes we watch everything. Zip, zip, zip, up and down the dial. It's magic.

If there are leftovers—a rare occurrence—I wrap them up and pack them away. I wash the dishes, and then finish up the night with more TV and homework. Sam dozes in front of the set. A good shoot-em-up will keep him awake, but not much else. The whole time we say hardly anything.

Homework from Eisenhower H.S., the educational truck stop of the Midwest. Sometimes I know everyone there—teachers, students, big shots—is just putting in time, waiting for their real lives to begin. At least Kathleen Marie O'Hare manages sometimes to teach as though life was about more than filling out forms and standing in line. She is at least interesting sometimes, and it is easier to forgive her for going off, which she still does on a regular basis. The rest of the day at Eisenhower is all crap and lies, smug rich white kids and deadly dull teachers. I swear to God, by the time Ohairy's class rolls around in the afternoon, if Todd weren't behind me all day, whispering to me to stay calm, assuring me I can survive even this awful place, there'd have been already many a dead Pinhead all over the high gloss floors of this tank.

I'm not all talk, you know.

O'Hare boasts of the deals she makes with the administration. Teach Tom Sawyer so they'll let you teach J. D. Salinger. Bullshit, right? I have the feeling she'll do what she damn well pleases. Regardless.

Many days even she goes on and on—with gerunds this and participles that—and many days I want to strangle her, too. But just when I make a ring of my hands and start to aim for her long pink neck, she opens a book and she reads in a voice that is almost hypnotic:

> The girl goes dancing there
> On the leaf-sown, new-mown, smooth
> Grass plot of the garden;
> Escaped from bitter youth,
> Escaped out of her crowd,
> Or out of her black cloud.
> Ah, dancer, ah, sweet dancer!

W. B. Yeats, she says. It's April. Look around: we are all in love with her, with life, with language and with love.

Well, for about five minutes, some of us are.

Tell me this broad doesn't always know exactly what she's doing. Still:

I find myself standing at her desk after class, ever-silent Todd dragging at my heels.

"Yes, Marshall," she says. She looks me in the eye and laughs.

"That poem . . ." I start, and see: she's already got me off balance.

"No one writes English like Yeats," she says. "Reading him you understand how our language should sound."

"Any other poets like that? Like me, I mean. Black. I figured if anyone would, you might know." I shrug my shoulders to let her off the hook in case she doesn't know. Also, you never let them think it's that important to you.

She sighs and makes this little face like she'd heard a rude noise in the room. "As a matter of fact, yes, there are wonderful poets of all nationalities," she says, and signals us to walk with her. "But you miss the point, Marshall."

As usual when dealing with this woman I am now humiliated. And thank God here's Todd, three steps behind and to the right should I vomit or something like that.

"You limit yourself. Life isn't black or white, and yet you react to everything as if it were. See me tomorrow during study hall and we'll talk more. Bring your watchdog too," she says, laughing, and – get this – Todd barks at her. Barks at her. She raises her eyebrows at him.

*

"You barked at a grown woman in a public place. Your brains have turned to shit." I say this to Todd, who's sitting there on the bus with his mouth hanging open and this silly half smile on his face. His cleft chin will be soaked over in drool at any moment.

"Poor boy's in love – hurting with it," Artie says. He is as bad as Betty Lou about this stuff. He reaches across the aisle with his foot to push Todd's knee, and he does it in a way that sickens me. Like a dirty old man on a bench would. All the same Todd exhales a ripe, mushy sigh, and I convince myself not to reach back there and slap him in his freckly face.

"Kathy, Kathy, Kathy." Todd says this looking off into the graffitied roof of the bus as if it were the Milky Way. "What a woman. I bet she's hotter than a firecracker: a regular seething volcano."

Artie, always a sucker for anything smutty out of Todd's mouth, almost falls off his chair, cackling at this nonsense.

"What is this shit?" I say. "You wouldn't know hot if your leg got fried off."

"I swear to God," Todd goes on in his reverie. "She reads another one of those purty love poems, my little peter's gonna come ripping right out of my jeans as big as life."

At which point I turn around and start whaling on him with my world history book, which happens to be the biggest thing I can get my hands on at the time. Quick, as if it were a reflex, he balls up to protect himself from the blows. I let him off with a light work over.

"Have mercy on the poor boy, Marsh. You can see he's in a bad way." Artie pulls me away before I work up a second wind.

"Get off me," I holler at sissy-boy.

"Please, Marsh," Todd begs. "Take me with you tomorrow. I'll be a little mouse in the corner. You won't even know I'm there." He says this after he's uncurled himself and had a chance to recover from the whooping I gave him.

I tell him, "You're fucked in the head, boy, is what your problem is. Especially if you think I'm going to spend my free hour with Ohairy. There's something wrong with that woman. She's trouble. You'll see."

"You're just afraid you'll learn something. You already know everything there is to know, right?" This is what Todd does—baits a person to get them to do what he wants. Todd and my mother. And maybe everyone else in the world.

"Tell him about himself," Artie says, getting his in. I swear: just like that Betty.

I say to Artie, "You keep your bald self out of this. And as for you," I point at Todd, "you'll be lucky if I don't turn around and give you some more of my fist."

Like Gandhi, Todd opens his arms, welcoming me to hurt him some more. Either he likes it or he's stupid.

*

And, so, of course, the next day, as we walk to Ohairy's room, I almost have to fire him up again over the smug look on his face.

"Don't say shit to me," I say.

We go into her office. Ohairy is the department head, so she gets her own office, but it's just a tiny little closet, really, as narrow as an alley with one tiny window way up high on the end of it. The whole thing looks smaller than it might because she has cluttered every space with books and papers. Plastering the walls are posters of various people such as Einstein and Alice Walker, and quotes from Emerson and from someone called Li Po.

"Welcome, boys," she says, and she offers us some chairs. So I take the one closest to her, putting Todd a little behind me. A good thing too, because when I look back there he's leaned back on the legs of the chair with his hands folded on his chest. He looks like the weasel that got into the hen house. I hope that his zipper hangs tough.

"What can I do for you fellows?" Ohairy says.

What is this shit: as I recall it, this meeting was her idea.

"I believe you have some things to discuss with Marshall," chimes in Todd, a person, mind you, who *never* says anything to anyone, except Artie and me, but around Ohairy is a regular chatterbox, even incorporating a full range of animal noises. I shoot him a look which I hope will turn him to stone, or at least those parts of him which aren't already rock hard.

"Forgive me, of course," she says. "I'm preoccupied . . . I'm glad you're here, Todd. You're so quiet, I don't know much about you. You really remind me of someone I know." She stops a minute, rubbing her chin, giving him the once over.

"Just take a look at this. See what I put up with," she says and passes me a letter of some kind. I hold the note at an angle which forces Romeo behind me to put his chair on the floor in order to see.

"Oh, you wanted to see this?" I query. Todd grabs my arm.

"Isn't that pathetic?" she asks.

All *I* see is this memo from her to the principal: something about starting a current events discussion club. At the bottom someone has written "We'll see." I'm completely lost, but Todd is shaking his head like an old dog in sympathy with — well, whatever it is we're supposed to be in sympathy with. I'm looking around for a bucket of cold water to douse him with.

"I'd join something like that," Todd says encouragingly. Then he asks me, "Why are you looking at me that way? I really would."

"Sure," I say. "Sure you would."

"Thank you, Todd. That's why I showed it to you. We need people like you boys around here. I think we could start some interesting things around here." Ohairy's color is almost as red as Todd by now. "Nevertheless, all the support I get around this . . . institution is, 'we'll see.'"

Somewhere between Yeats and now I've gotten lost.

"I'm sorry about your little club," I say, and from behind me I hear a gasp and my name said as if I'd just picked my nose in public or something. A sharp index fingernail stabs pointedly at my chest.

"Which reminds me of your poets," She backs up by the door. She's got one hand on her tailored, gray-suited hip and the sharp finger still pointed in my direction.

"I thought about what you asked me for. I decided to loan you this." She hands me a book. It is called *Voices of the World*. "It's a big world out there. Not just about blacks and whites, or Marshall Finney. Or me, or Todd either."

Todd has leaned forward now, resting his elbows on his knees nodding in solemn agreement. I decide right then that he will be paying for this attitude at a later date.

She carries on. "The whole world could blow up at any time. Instant death for everyone. Aren't you boys absolutely scared to death? I know I am. And these preppies out here! . . . So ignorant! So self-involved!"

I try to figure out what the hell she's talking about so I can plan which look to get on my face: shock? indignation? retardation? I look at Todd. Thin-skinned, sweet Todd: he's blinking back tears.

Miss Jane Fonda O'Hare works up to her big finish. "Can't we at least talk about this stuff at this school? Just — maybe — it's not too late and — maybe — we can make a real difference. And," she snatches the memo back, "I'm going right now to talk to someone about starting our discussion group."

"I'd like to come, too," says Todd.

Just like that the two of them are out the door.

"Join us, Marshall," Ohairy says over her shoulder.

I decline.

I'm left sitting there as the two of them blaze off in their passionate fury. So I figure I'll talk to the plants. "Hey, plants," I say, "I'm interested in important things as much as the next person. As much as a person with my life is able to be."

Then I figure I better clear out of Ohairy's office before I get accused of stealing something.

*

On the bus back home Todd's sullen window-staring takes on a new intense coloring; something more than self-pity perhaps.

38

He comes to long enough to speak to me. "I think we'll get our club," he says.

"Gods be praised." I answer.

"This is important, Marsh," he whispers.

I nod begrudgingly, giving him his due. Sweet Todd: Peace on Earth, bless his heart, that'll be the only piece he gets.

*

Item by item, I pack away Rose's life. Sneakily at first, starting with things like the pea-sized ceramic unicorns she collected as if they were gold dust. The little hand-painted poodles, too. Actually, what I do first is to pull the cheap mystery novels off the shelf and tear out the last chapter. I get into a rhythm, ripping to the beat of the videos. Then I figure, "what the hell," she'd already read them anyway, so I save the energy and just pitch them. Not even someone like her rereads mysteries. Some things were so disgusting: I threw away all of these eighty-nine-cent nail polishes in ridiculous colors like raspberry frost and lilac mist. Imagine having a mother who wears the same nail polish as the sophomore class president.

So, I'm cleaning and the phone rings and it's her.

"Marshall," she says, "it's me."

I don't say a word.

"I didn't expect this to be so hard," she says.

"Sam's not home from work."

"I know. I know that," she says. "Lord, don't tell me when my own husband works."

There is a long pause, a lot of static on the line.

"Um, Marshall. I've got some things figured out. I want to tell them to you."

"Your things?"

"I want you to listen to me."

"You want me to send your things to you?"

There's only some sort of breathing on the line.

"I'll send them to your family," I say, and then there's only some more of that breathing filling the silence. So I hang up.

Right then and there I decide to let her crap rot right on the hangers. Let the moths eat each and every stitch.

I stash only the eyesores: ugly beige and brown rocks that serve no purpose, plastic beads, stamps torn from the corners of envelopes—the doo-hickeys that gather dust on every possible place they can perch in this, our . . . my house. I pack her memory from view so that Big Sam and I can rest easy.

After which comes the call from Aunt Lucille.

"Marshall, no silly stuff," she says, "I'm coming to get some things for your mother."

"You'll have to talk to Sam."

"I'm talking to you," she says.

I learned young you don't mess around with Ms. Lucille Robinson. A little seven-year-old boy I once knew told her more or less to mind her own business. She fired his little behind up real good—so good I think it's still stinging to this day.

What else you don't do is put Sam Finney in the same room with Lucille, at least not without police escort, you don't. The former Lucille Diggs and her sisters, my aunts and now dead grandma, are big light-skinned women—black women with blond and red hair—who fought their way to big money jobs in stuff like social work, and they'll be happy to tell you that they didn't take no crap from nobody getting there.

"Yes, ma'am," I says to Aunt Lucille on the phone. I tell her to come and do it now, quick, before Sam gets home from work.

*

Lucille packs everything away, even things I've neglected. I help her to load it into her Lincoln. What she doesn't take we fill with mothballs and cram into the crawlspace above the kitchen. Artie and Todd are there, standing by, playing chess, watching "Star Trek." Lucille gives them the evil eye because she's got "some things she wants to discuss." Nothing you'd discuss in front of "company."

"Wouldn't be no sitting around were this my house," she says.

"It's not," I mumble.

She grabs the fleshy part of my ear and twists. "I'll deal with you later. You know what I'm talking about, don't you?"

I can only relax after she's gone and the deed's done. The boys and I have a good laugh. Out of sight, out of mind.

*

That night I can feel Sam's eyes on my back.

"Marshall, come here."

I follow him to the bedroom. The drawers to the dressers stand open. So do the sliding closet doors.

"Where are they?" he says. He says it in a strange, quiet voice.

My eyes follow the sculptured patterns on the bedroom rug. Around and around it goes.

"Look at me. What did you do? Tell me." He shoves me back out the door just hard enough that I bounce into the wall. He starts yelling. "I asked you a question. You know so damned much."

He snatches a handful of his own clothes from the closet. He hurls them at me. In a shower the rags fall around me.

"Well?" he demands.

I retreat toward the living room.

"You're the big man. What have you done?" he yells.

I see him behind me in the curlicue mirror, opening the linen closet, emptying towels and soap and toilet paper, kicking it, throwing it. The steam iron sails over my shoulder cracking my reflection. Suddenly there are hundreds of Marshalls.

In the kitchen he smashes plates. He sweeps cans and canisters to the floor with a single swipe across a shelf or a counter. All the time screaming, "What have you done? What have you done?"

Sitting on the couch, I cower beneath my arms, my head down on my knees. I can hear myself. I'm chanting.

"I'm sorry."

"I'm sorry."

"I'm sorry."

Big Sam stands over me. His whole body shakes. His face and arms are shiny wet. Both hands vibrate. He clenches them in fists by the side of his head. Tightly clenched. They resemble large brown hams.

"What did you do?" he says. A whisper.

A voice from the door says, "The boy didn't do nothing. I did."

Then Aunt Lucille says, "Touch him. Go on. There'll be a new face in hell tomorrow morning. My guarantee. Something told me . . . God it was told me . . . Lucille Robinson, turn this car around, your family is in need. Praise his holy name. And have mercy on your soul Sam Finney if you move another muscle."

The fists drop. A big swollen hand reaches in my direction.

"Don't. Don't you dare," Lucille says.

"I might have figured on you," he says. His voice is full of remorse and defeat and fatigue. He stumbles through the piles of linen and towels down the hallway. He closes the door to his room behind him.

Lucille stands above me at my back, gently rubbing my shoulder, watching him go. She bends low and says in a voice like honey, "I guess I saved your butt. This time."

5

THE NEXT MORNING Sam says to Lucille, "I see you're still here."

Obviously. She has made herself a lovely nest right on the green-plaid sofa using some of the linens Sam so graciously distributed for her.

"Thought I'd visit with my nephew a few days, if you don't mind." She is real cool and casual about this.

"If I did?" mumbles Sam.

I get a good look at Lucille. She is frightful. Her yellowish skin has blotches of pink here and there where the buttons on the couch stabbed her in the night. Her thick reddish-colored Afro stands at attention around her head in matted clumps. She has draped herself in a floral printed sheet of unfortunate greens and pinks, made it into a toga-like thing. Like a clown she looks, or like Miss Liberty herself, due to the spatula that's upright in one hand like a torch.

"Who are you looking at with a face like that?" she says to me. "Best get these eggs while the getting's good."

"Yes, ma'am," I say. Big Sam shakes his head in disgust. He gets in his pickup truck and disappears for the day.

*

Saturday.

Sam's been making himself scarce during Lucille's stay. Lucille has scrubbed, baked, and washed her way from one end of the crackerbox to the other.

Lucille is a widow woman, or that's what Sam calls her. In fact she has put three husbands in the ground in her fifty years and, also according to Big Sam, is not without a gentleman friend for too long, even these days. She must be between engagements at present. Lucille has a big rambling house in the Central West End, which Rose always describes as a showplace and, also according to Rose, the delivery trucks from Famous-Barr never stop coming after a sale, so well-set financially is she from the various deceased cohabitors of the so-called showplace. Ask Lucille what she does for a living, though, and mysteriously the husbands disappear. She tells you she is something called a churchwoman — out here doing the Lord's work. This evidently has something to do with delivering meals and ministering to the sick and shut-in, and is somehow associated with the congregation of the Union-Central West Missionary Full Gospel Tabernacle with which Lucille has been affiliated for going on a dozen years — ever since her rebirth from heathendom during a notoriously rowdy family picnic in Forest Park.

The Lord's work apparently also leaves you time to move in with relatives as needed.

"Now we've got this house straightened up and respectable, we'll have time to visit," she says. I quick get on the phone and get Artie and Todd over here for the day.

*

"Aren't you a couple of nice young men," Lucille says to them. "Tell me: do your mamas really allow sitting up in other folks' houses all day?"

To which Artie says "Oh, no, ma'am, Miss Lucille. We sure are pleased to have been invited to spend some time with you today."

I wink to let him know this is just the kind of crap I want dished out.

Lucille says "My, my, isn't this a polite gentleman. You can certainly tell who's had a proper upbringing around here." I can tell she is also admiring Barbie's doll clothes. Old Artie grins from ear to ear.

I indicate with my mouth to ignore Lucille, which for some reason is so funny to the boys that they snicker right in her face. Lucille is nothing if not gracious. She sets about in the kitchen to make us some lunch.

On Rose's dinette table she lays a yellow polka-dotted tablecloth, which she must keep in her purse, because I've never in my life seen it around this house. Then she sets four places to which she calls us in from the TV where we are playing Mario Brothers. I want to finish the game, but I am assured by Artie that would not be polite. He makes his point by turning off the set.

When we get settled, she places at each seat a tumbler of iced tea with a lemon wedge straddling the rim. Then she puts down a plate on which an elaborate lunchmeat sandwich has been arranged between some slices of tomato and a mound of freshly made potato salad. Even a sprig of parsley (or some other kind of green stuff) sprouts out of the salad like a miniature tree in a yellow desert.

I'm really impressed with all of this food, all of the trouble she's gone to. So much so, I go to take a big swig off the iced tea, which is about the most refreshing looking thing I've seen in ages. Just then, there is a sharp stinging slap on my hand.

"Marshall Field Finney, how much of a heathen are you, child?" Lucille clamps the errant arm to the table, pinning it with her own iron claw. I feel like a porcupine caught in a steel trap.

"Who will now give thanks to Lord Jesus for the bountiful blessings of this day?" she asks.

"Might I?" offers Artie. He catches my eye to see if I see the gleam in his.

"Young man, what's your name, Arthur? Please to bless our meal at this time."

Artie takes off in this high falutin tone that sounds like Jesse Jackson, or something. He works in all the right "heavenly fathers" and "we thank you humblies," and "in-the-name-ofs," and the whole time I'm pulling back with all of my might on the clamped arm. Lucille doubles her strength to assure my continued capture.

Finally, there is a hearty amen. Without warning my own hand is set free and snaps up almost slapping me in my own face.

"Bless your heart," Lucille says to Artie, and he gets this "aw shucks ma'am" look on his face, for which I kick him good and hard in the shins.

"Shoot, Marshall," he says. He acts as if his leg's broke in two, which it would have been if I'd wanted it to be, but didn't. "You play too much," he whines.

"Shame on you—treating guests so," Lucille scolds. "You gentlemen enjoy your lunches. Don't pay this heathen here no mind," and then to Todd she says, "You sure got a head of red hair on you," which is as much as she ever says to him. As if he were some sort of big white baby doll or something. All the same, Todd gets to blushing bright red.

"This is a lovely lunch you've prepared, Miss Lucille," says Artie. Just then I have a whole mouth full of chewed sandwich. I open my mouth in his direction so he can get a good look at it.

Lucille gives him this "no-trouble-at-all" pat on the hand and tells him to help himself because there is plenty more. Saying that to Artie and Todd is pretty much the same thing as giving Dracula a free pass to the blood bank. I've about lost all appetite at this point, so I sit back and glare across the table at the Hoover twins who have inhaled every morsel of food laid before them.

"Look at that face on that boy," Lucille says of me to Artie and Todd. Then to me she says, "Your face'll freeze in that position and you'll never catch a wife."

"Huh," I say (– a great comeback!) Artie and Todd think this is the funniest thing in the world and are almost sick with laughter.

I am relieved when finally Lucille asks if anbody wants anything else. She asks this after frick and frack have already eaten two bowls of chocolate chip ice cream and about drained a gallon of iced tea. Already little pot bellies have popped out on each of them as if they were knocked up. They wisely beg off more of anything.

"Well, then," says Lucille, grabbing one elbow of each and lifting them from the table. "It's been lovely, and I guess you youngsters will be on your way. You must come and visit again soon."

Before I am able to protest – which I might not anyway, considering the shameless way our boys have carried on – Lucille is ushering them through the living room and wishing them a good day. I believe this is what's known as the bum's rush. She waves to them from the porch.

"Little old red-haired thing," she purrs. She turns to me. "Now we'll have time for that little talk."

"Shit," I say under my breath. I have no intention of talking or listening for that matter.

"I heard that," she answers. She orders me to empty out the dryer, indicating that she will iron while I fluff and fold.

No rest for the wicked.

*

"Those are nice friends you have there. So mannerly and refined."

Even at the state penitentiary they behave when fed. I don't say this out loud, of course.

"Kind of long hair on that one. The white one. But a sweet boy all the same. And your other friend — what was his name?"

"Attila?" I say.

"Yes, Arthur. Such a fine young man. I figure there's hope for you yet with such friends as this."

What am I: an axe murderer? I don't say this either.

After a period of folding and fluffing, Lucille says, "Rosie told me about your little stunt on the phone." She dumps a load of folded towels off the chair and orders me to do them over again. The right way.

"Don't bother saying anything," she says. "Just listen to me good. This here is Sam and Rose's business. It's none of your concern. You understand me? Do you?"

"Yes, ma'am," I say, really quiet.

"Like this, fool," she says. She grabs a towel and shows me the Lucille Robinson method. She makes a full-sized bath towel into a compact rectangle as hard as a brick and only a little larger. "Practice that," she orders.

"You're lucky — can you imagine?" she goes on. "What if your daddy found out? Don't worry about me. I won't say a word — but I should. Don't thank me, either. I've know Sam Finney too long. You'd be laid out in a coffin, arms crossed in a new blue suit. You know that, too. Don't you?"

"Yes ma'am."

"Mr. Sam Finney. What on earth it was, attracted my baby to that? He was what you call the silent type. Didn't say nothing unless absolutely need be. A ladies' man. Everybody knew about him. Walking around with two or three heifers at once. Never seen nothing like it in my life. A dog." She stops long enough to crack open a window, to say there's never enough air in these cheap houses.

"You have to forgive me, baby. Talking about you daddy. But never in my life had I seen a man so . . . mannish. It was hardly civililized, if you ask me. But then no one did. Wouldn't you know, Rose hadn't met him too long, and there they were up and getting married."

She goes on and on. The best I can remember, something as follows:

"Desmond and Shirley — rest my sweet sister's soul — had that Sam over for supper, I recall, and all of us relatives, too. Rosie was no more than eighteen at the time." Lucille moves the iron back and forth in a rhythmic rocking. She takes a long drink of iced tea, swallowing it slowly, as if the tea were as thick as tar. On she goes:

"They were nervous you understand—him being twenty-four and what you call already an experienced man. Sam Finney sat there not saying a word. But do you know he never took his eyes off that girl all night. Like he expected her to vanish in thin air or something. Her sitting there all shy, but lighting up the room, anyway.

"Put those towels in the linen closet. Do it right and none of your monkey business. And get me some more iced tea: this iron's like to got me on fire."

I do this and I do that. Just as I'm told. I check the dryer for lost socks. I check the time as well. Surely the boys have already left for the movies. Here's Lucille going on and on about everything in the ancient world.

"Marshall," she says to me. "You must have some shirts to iron for school."

"My clothes don't need ironing," I tell her.

"Don't need it, huh." She sets the iron up. It whistles as the steam rushes out. "Look at what nice well-kept things your friend wears."

"Barbie." I say.

"Yes, Arthur—he makes a nice appearance indeed. As does your mama. Back in those days Rosie was a high-spirited thing. She'd set every occasion to life with her laugh and with those eyes. Strong-willed. No one told her what to do. Have you ever heard your mama sing, Marshall?"

"No, ma'am," I say, and then I realize that that might not be true. Surely I'd have heard her sing sometime. There must have been a time when she was happy, and how could I have forgotten that? "I mean, I guess I don't remember," I say, changing my story.

"Yes, you do too remember, Marshall Finney. Back then she had a full, warm voice. Just like the late Miss Mahalia Jackson, rest her soul. Smooth and mellow like a warm afternoon. Rose sang all the time: Love songs and the Lord's praise."

I have this strange mix of anger and emptiness because I don't hear anything at all. I decide I'd better meet the boys at the show: maybe it's not too late. This has gone on too long.

"I'm gonna call some friends," I say.

"Sit," she says. "Your friends'll keep. I might not."

So I sit. Maybe I'll fetch, roll over, and play dead too.

*

"That's why I objected, you see," Lucille drones on. She is now mending hems, sewing on buttons. "To the marriage, that is. My girl, so full of life. With that man. I knew he'd drive every ounce of spirit from her. I knew it. May the Lord have mercy on his soul."

I sit there on the couch for a long time waiting for the next pronouncement. I try to imagine Sam and Rose back in those days. Young Rose, not much older than me, maybe at a party or a dance. Sam, hair all black, dressed in some fancy stud clothes, maybe in tangerine-colored pants and red shoes. They might be slow dancing to a record by Smokey Robinson and the Miracles. Or maybe they have gone to Rose's prom. Sam has pinned a too-large orchid on her lemon-yellow formal dress.

They are no one I know, but, then where am I anyway? Where is Marshall in all of this?

"Marshall," Lucille says, sitting beside me and placing a hand on my arm. She has turned on the bowling tournament. It is right here we'll sit until dinnertime. "Marshall you never have asked me about her." A chubby man in a peach-colored shirt rolls two strikes. "You want to know—I'm sure you do. Ask me about her."

Then there are some beer commercials.

"You want to know where she is. Ask me."

"She did what she wanted. She left. That's where she is." A man in a red shirt is angry because he has two spares in a row. Big money rides on every ball. This is what bowling is like. One ball and then another and then another. Every time there is a strike Lucille and I pop up like toast. Meanwhile her hand pets my arm.

"This isn't about you, Marshall," she says.

She knows nothing. A dried-up childless busybody. "Let's watch the game," I say.

"You're so much alike." She says. "You'd've liked my Rosie a lot."

As if she were someone I didn't know.

*

Sunday morning, everybody in Washington Park knows they better let Marshall sleep. So I'm plenty pissed when here's Lucille got up in what looks like a nurse's uniform, only blue, and a hat with some sort of little net up front, announcing it's time for church. Church is the last place I had intended being on this particular day.

"It's late. We can't get to Union Gospel," I say into my pillow. I am content that that's that, and she's discouraged.

"Get up, I said. For your information Full Gospel runs continuous services all day Sunday, every Sunday." She says this in a way too spirited for almost any basic sentence.

"I aim to check out the preaching right here at Park Baptist. Ten A.M. Which gives you a full twenty-five minutes to get presentable."

I groan and pull the covers over my head.

"I'm waiting," she bellows.

A new voice chimes in: Big Sam's. "Get up and go," he orders.

Swell. Double-teamed, on a Sunday, no less. I get it together, though. This involves peeling a navy blue suit out of its cleaning bag. Sam spins me around checking for tags. Then he straightens my tie. I notice he's got canary feathers all over his face.

"What are you smirking at?" I ask.

He whispers, "I'd like to see this show myself." He propels me in the direction of the door where Lucille waits. She is carrying a shiny blue handbag the size of a hatbox. Martians could live in this purse. Here I am going out in public with a woman toting a giant-sized glow-in-the-dark purse.

"Twins," she says, holding her sleeve next to mine, and then she says to Sam, "Sam Finney! Your heathen soul needs saving, too. You best get in line with the rest of us sinners."

"See you in hell, Lucille."

*

At least Park Baptist is peaceful: A boy can get in a good nap there. Park Baptist is Reverend Alan T. William's church—Reverend Alan T. Williams, that's the way he introduces himself, oily hand extended. You'd think every Sunday here was the Academy Awards, too, the way everybody's looking around to see who's there and who's not there.

You should see them when Rose struts in, wearing some silky red dress, a wide-brimmed lid shading her eyes, this holier-than-thou-art look on her face. A couple of these old sisters near have strokes. Thank God Rose only shows up twice a year.

I always have to remind myself that the point of all this church mess is so as not to burn in hell.

Rev. Williams is pretty cool, though. He knows what keeps the money coming in.

Sometimes Rev reads a poem, after which there is always singing and a prayer. Once, in a sermon, Rev told us how hard it was to get service in some of the larger department stores. He reminded us that as Christians our patience is tried at every turn, yet we must learn to abide. He told us to call the manager and complain.

This is information that people can use. None of that hellfire mess. Apparently everyone in the Park agrees. Rev. Williams gets bought a new Cadillac with some frequency. Last year the deacons paved the lot so as he could park it on nice, fresh asphalt.

Lucille and I arrive just after ten at the end of the organ processional. It very well could be the moving conclusion of Prince's "Purple Rain" for all I know. That's not unlikely either considering the organist, sister Lonnée Evans, plays electric piano evenings in a said to be up-and-coming multi-racial rock-and-soul outfit of local origin.

Lucille picks a fairly central pew. Just two rows ahead of us I spy Artie, perched between Miss Ida and Betty. Each of them is dressed to the nines. Artie turns around and waves, catching Lucille's eye. She gives him an audible "Hi, sugar," and, to me, says, "There's your little friend," all of this just as Rev. Williams pulls up to the pulpit to start his sermon.

"Good morning, brothers and sisters," he begins. There is a polite echo of "mornings" to him. "Shall we pray?"

We all bow our heads, but when I look down I notice I am wearing one green sock and one blue one. So does Lucille. Her mouth falls open and a half-done Lifesaver rolls out of her onto the floor – a disaster because now she will have to fish through the enormous space capsule purse to locate another one.

Rev prays. He talks to God as if he were a close friend or a poker buddy. Rev talks to everyone that way. That's how one probably ought to talk to God. One also ought to assume that God is not hard of hearing, using what you'd call a reasonable tone not the siren-like howl you get in some of these places. Rev finishes with a quiet "amen," which is echoed everywhere almost silently. Except to my left where there is a hearty "AMEN, PRAISE HIM," loud enough to wake the dead.

Sneaky Artie turns around and back so fast that even I almost don't catch the grin on his face.

Rev. Williams, a well-known vegetarian in these parts, selects for his subject this Sunday the "preciousness and sanctity of all of God's creations" — fairly heavy-duty business for a place such as Washington Park. Rev believes that just because you ain't rich, doesn't mean you have to have an immoral diet. According to Artie — who you will find every Sunday in that same pew between Betty Lou and Miss Ida — his anti-meat sermon is an annual favorite, timed not coincidently to open National Eat More Pork month, the signs for which fill every wall of Miss Ida's store with gleeful pink pigs. Needless to say this sermon creates a bit of tension between Miss Ida and the Rev. And why are those pigs smiling anyway?

He starts off slowly — with a story about how he had many childhood pets that he loved, as, he is sure, did many of the congregation's young people. At this point many of the church members shift their weight and dig around absent-mindedly in their clothes. Lucille gets a round, open-mouthed expression on her face, which is either confusion or disbelief. Maybe both.

Lucille's right with him, though. Appreciating it, too. She begins nodding in agreement about five minutes into it. Finding a thread of some sort to follow, she adds "praise him," "uh huh," and a moan to her responses.

Rev builds to an albeit subdued crescendo. "So I say to you my friends that in every leaf on every tree . . ."

The voice on my left comes in with a loud "Yes sir."

Rev halts, looks stunned, but only for a second because he's finally got some life out of this crowd, and on his favorite sermon, too. He's gonna go with it.

"In the smallest sparrow . . ."

"Yes, sir."

". . . the largest animal that roams the great forest . . ."

"Tell it, sir."

I can feel eyes all over the room on us and up ahead Artie and Betty are nudging each other deep in the pew.

". . . yes, in all of these God has placed his spirit, placed the very essence of life."

"Praise him."

I look over at her, but she is wrapped completely in the sermon.

"Let us rejoice . . ."

"Hallelujah."

". . . let us rejoice, I say . . ."

"Hallelujah."

Rev's voice is one octave and several decibals above normal. Here and there new voices join the call and response.

". . . let us rejoice in his presense."

"Yes, yes."

The room seems to buzz and glow. My face is burning, so I look down.

"Let the manifestation of his presence . . ."

"Go on now." Even Artie and company beam and join in.

". . . let it fill our hearts."

"Fill our hearts."

"Let us strive every day in every way to appreciate, preserve, and protect: let us love all of his gifts of life."

"Amens" all around as Lonnée draws out the first chord of "Jesus Dropped the Charges." As we sing Lucille grabs my left hand and clutches it tightly in hers. I am crying, though I don't know why. Perhaps because my fingers are being crushed.

As the plate passes Lucille presses a dollar into my hand, squeezes it so that the bill drops out automatically, then passes the plate herself. This is surely the best haul Rev's seen in months: dollar bills ooze over the edges of the plate.

Finally the whole mess concludes with a heartfelt prayer: there is even applause at the end. Lonnée strikes up what could be "Zippidy Doo Da" for all I know.

There's Rev at the portal huggin, kissin, and blessin up a storm. Everyone tells him he was never better, volunteering for the shut-in program and for youth activity night. All of them promise to be back next week and forever. Lucille, waiting to greet him, is waving and blessing everyone in every direction. The congregation waves and blesses her in return. They even pat me on the back. I am held hostage, my arm hooked through hers, my hand locked in a white-gloved vice.

When it's our turn to greet the Williamses, I am reminded of my manners and make the formal presentation.

"Reverend and Mrs. Alan T. Williams: this is my aunt, Mrs. Lucille Robinson."

They receive her as visiting royalty. Lucille praises Rev for his inspirational service — praises him to the point I expect her to get down on all fours and kiss his feet. This his annual animal protection sermon, no less.

"Miss Robinson, you have graced our sanctuary. Marshall, you must bring your aunt to us again."

Lucille bows deeply, discharging another Lifesaver from her mouth.

Up ahead, Sister Ida and clan wait at the parking lot. Warm greetings are exchanged by all. There is an extra measure of praise for Mr. Arthur Warner, who today is dressed as if he were the best man in Barbie's wedding party. Sister Ida invites us home for fried chicken and glazed ham (sorry Rev), potatoes, and green beans cooked in salt pork. We pick up Sam and make it an afternoon.

Since I have had it with Queen-for-the-day Lucille, and am not speaking to a certain Arthur Warner, who has turned into a regular Little Lord Fauntleroy prick, I park myself between Sam and Sister Ida. Sister Ida spends dinner praising Jesus with Lucille.

On the other side of me Big Sam and Betty are chortling and giggling and picking off each other's plates. Sam tears huge hunks off a drumstick. He finishes it off in two bites. He is grunting with pleasure. Betty Lou smacks her lips in delight.

Sam, using this big deep laugh not heard in months, saying "Mmm, mmm, mmm, Miss Betty, you sure nough fry up a good chicken."

"Hush your mouth, Big Sam," Betty says.

Suddenly I find myself in a goddamn Crisco commercial.

Shortly after some hot peach cobbler and vanilla ice cream, I stand up and announce I've got homework. Artie shakes his head "no," as if it were important to him that I stay, but I hit the door at practically a run. Not surprisingly no one comes after me. So they sit up there doing Lord knows what the rest of the afternoon.

*

After her big day, Lucille goes to soak in a hot tub. When he comes home, Big Sam stops by my room. I am lying back checking out the ceiling. I pick out one place and stare. It becomes a hole, starts pulsing and rolling in my direction like hyperspace in the movies. Or I am rolling into it. From somewhere out there I here Sam talking.

"Quite a meal we had there," he says.

"Yes, sir."

He gets a hanger on which to hang the good blue blazer he's taken out of mothballs just for today. The coat hardly closes at the middle anymore.

"I understand we had quite a church service this morning, too. Sorry I missed that." Sam chuckles for the second time in months.

"It's not funny," I say. "She floorshowed. I'll never even be able to show my face . . ."

"Boy, you're so full of shit," Sam says. He goes and changes into some overalls. "Let me tell you something," he says on his return. "Didn't nobody know you was there. Bless her meddlesome old soul, she loves her Jesus."

"She's driving me crazy. I wish she'd leave."

Sam shrugs. "Not my problem," he says.

I sit up. I ask what he means.

"She sure ain't here to see me," he says. "You got to be a man, son. Sometimes you got to be a man." He just walks away. He dumps it all on me. And, that's the last he'll say of it, too. I know.

*

As I hug Aunt Lucille at the end of the next week, she squeezes me as if she wanted all of the life to leave me. She rubs me on the head and she looks at me, her green eyes all watered over. She says, "You'll be just fine, so don't fret."

Sam watches out the door not saying anything while I load what little she'd come with into the big Lincoln.

Was I afraid Lucille was made of glass? Did I expect her to fall apart like a cheap toy? All you know to do sometimes is what's best for you. For me, I decided Lucille had better go.

When I told her, she was in the kitchen scrubbing at a stain in the sink.

"Maybe Sam and I will be okay," I said. Which means only that she was never gonna work out whatever problems there were between him and me. I know it wasn't news to her.

Lucille raised her head high and faced me. "Well, I guess I can be moving on," she'd said, almost dry-eyed. She said it almost with a smile.

I cried, patting my fingers under my eyes because I didn't want to be crying. I couldn't look at her.

She pulled me to her, insisted I was right and it was time she left. I wanted to die.

Out of the car window she says to me "You'll always have a home with me. Anytime. Tell me you know that. Say it to me."

"I know," I say, and I do know. I bet myself right there that even the worst person in the world, greased up and ready to fry in the electric chair, has an Aunt Lucille telling him he's okay. And even if you accidentally gave her the finger as they grilled you, which would make the last thing you did in life flipping the old girl off, she'd be at your grave to see you off to your eternal damnation. There, just because you are someone she loves.

As she pulls away I smile despite myself and feel incredibly safe, indestructible.

I turn around and shrug. Big Sam shrugs back.

The next day a postcard addressed to me waits in the mail. A picture of downtown Las Vegas at night. It says:

Marshall,
  Everything will be okay. I can feel it.
  Trust me.

Mother

*

Can you imagine? Part of being a Finney is never knowing what to think.

6

SOMETIMES IN THE summer, when we were smaller — what Big Sam called little sawed-off runts — the boys and I would sneak up Dorset Road, hop the fence, and go poking around in the old gravel pit. You might find anything in the landfill or at least we thought we might: diamonds, gold, arrows, trinkets from lost civilizations. You couldn't tell us then there wasn't anything there but crushed sandstone, that this was only a garbageman's dream.

I'd boost little Todd up, he'd grab hold of Artie, and we'd roll over the fence like ants crossing a stream. This was until we discovered ourselves a hole low in the fence that some previous explorers had dug. Todd always kicked a few rocks underneath first. He'd decided that this was the sort of place copperheads liked. At the time the landfill was still mostly a quarry, more gravel than rats.

Most often we'd start off the day land skiing and sledding.

Here's how: You run up a little hill and then take off skidding until you start an avalanche that carries you down with it.

Then someone would notice a pretty stone, maybe the color of a shrimp, or maybe pointed like a spear tip. So everybody'd be digging around to find his own. We'd see that our diggings looked like cave villages, or like cities in the desert. We'd build roads and canals in the soft sands to connect our kingdoms, roads that coiled and wound around like snakes. After a soaking rain you could even make tunnels in the hills.

Then someone would misstep and smash-up someone else's stuff. Sometimes on purpose. What else could a boy do but declare war, bitter wars, fought with great clumps of rock and missiles of sandstone as light as feathers.

"Cr-crck-cruck, splatt, boom, pish," our whiny voices made the sounds of heavy artillery. Miraculously all sides surrendered in exhaustion long before feelings got hurt, or a too well-aimed salvo found its mark.

Here would be three sweaty, dust-caked boys panting in the gravel pit, two burnt black and the other bright red by the midwest summer sun. Until we remembered it was suppertime, scurried back down the hollow, forgetting even to kick rocks under the fence hole. One mamma or the other would want to know where you'd gotten so scruffy, so ashy.

"We was just playing," we'd say.

When Big Sam got wind of us in the landfill, that bout put an end to our little visits. He said he didn't want to hear ever again as long as he drew breath of us playing in no trash pit. He about tore up two little black butts, and would have torn up a red one, too, had he been sure how those people 'cross the tracks would have taken it.

We learned our lesson, believe it or not, and the closest we'd gone since was to linger at the fence, longingly watching the last gravel go, watching the hole fill up with plastic milk jugs and lifeless refrigerators.

Never once had I gone to the landfill with Big Sam.

*

On a Saturday morning after school was out, Big Sam's at my door saying to me "Get dressed," which I do. The sun is barely over the top of the hill, the sky still streaked with gray, rose, and hot gold. We load in the pickup with a thermos of coffee and go rolling up Dorset toward Colerain Road. The brown Dodge pickup already sparkles in the morning light, so well-shined is she. In the back of the truck Sam lays blankets and tarps so the bed never gets scratched up by the junk he collects.

I am surprised that rather than go out Colerain to wherever, we pull off into the landfill. Sam gets out, so I take my cue and get out too. He leans back on the fender, by the headlamp, and pours himself a coffee. I climb up on the hood and slide back. My butt makes a loud squeaking sound against the metal. I lean on the windshield.

"You risking death, boy," he says, giving me a mock-fierce look. He checks for scratches, and then offers me some coffee, which I decline. He swats my tennis-shoed feet off the edge of the hood, off to the side so that they hang in space.

The morning air is chilly, but you can already tell it'll be a hot one. Sam stares out over the landfill as if it were the Grand Canyon. Above me some scraggly scavenger birds circle.

Sam sips on the steaming coffee. "We're almost full," he says. "Maybe another year's worth, if that."

"Then what?" I ask.

"Cover it up. Bury it and forget it."

"Just like that?" I ask, flatly—more a statement, to make conversation.

Sam pours himself some more coffee. "Down south, I think it was twenty years ago, they had a hole that they buried up. Landscaped it and built houses on top. Nice houses. Time goes by and some of that gas backs up. These holes get full of gas. That mess liked to blow the whole place sky high."

Sam laughs and I laugh with him.

"Really," he says. "This here is most all clean fill—not too much garbage, but who knows what folks sneak in here at night. Won't be my problem, I guess."

"What are you gonna do?"

"When we're full?" He shrugs. "Something. At least I'll be free of it."

Sam scans his domain and gets part of a smile across his face. "We used to own all of this," he says. "All this land come to the Finneys after the Civil War. All this raggedy hollow land down to the tracks. Apple orchards and grapes. You still see those fruit trees, don't you?"

"Yes, sir," I say, but I haven't seen anything except for a few crab-apple trees and some sour green grapes climbing fences.

"My grandpa wasn't much for knocking apples, nor for scaring up vegetables from some damn rocky hill. He must've been scratching out here one day, hit something hard and dreamed up this: a rock pile. Mr. Samuel Finney Jr.'s Rock and Gravel company. The 'colored quarry' they called it."

Sam sees a box of cans someone left by the big shed which sits facing Dorset road. The shed serves as office and warehouse and garage. He goes over and sorts the cans into one of his recycling bins. Sam can be very organized. All around this dump stuff stands, stacks, piles, or gathers according to category: washing machines here, dead cars there. When you think you got the system figured, like magic a whole pile disappears.

Sam comes back and empties the thermos.

"Yep, they made good money out of this hole. Good money. You'd never know it walking back down the hollow. Niggers living in shacks, lean-tos—some no more than caves. Clean, mind you. Yes sir, them was clean folks back then.

"My daddy tells he went into one joint. The floor was shiny like you'd never believe. Daddy says he'd never seen no linoleum that color. Boy with him says, 'Fool, that's dirt.' Shiny as a new penny, Daddy said."

"Come on," I say. When Big Sam and his cronies get going you have to remember everything's got a little embroidery around it.

"I'm just telling you what my daddy told me," he says. "Daddy knew all them old folks down there. He was born here. This was his. Ours."

"Until?"

Sam moves his big hands through his hair, sighs and sputters. The sun, already high enough to warm the windshield, sparkles on a bend in the river that I can see in the distance. You only see that river from up here certain times of the day—like early morning and sunset. Sam catches the sparkle too, I can tell, and watches it until it disappears.

"So much bullshit. So much you'll never know," he says. "Let's walk." We go ambling along, surrounded by rows of old rubber tires and stacks of rusted appliances. Sam carries a pointed stick, maybe to gather stray garbage, maybe to spear rats with.

"Think about it," he says. "We emptied this old hole, now filled her back up again. Seems fitting, don't it? Take and give back."

"I remember," I tell him, "when this was like a big canyon."

"And I'm sure you remember how I wore out your little bottom for playing up in it. Stop right here," he says.

We arrive on a rise of almost white clay studded here and there with cans, boards, and the bottoms of green glass bottles. A hot wind rustles our pants legs.

"What do you do with a big empty hole in the ground?" Big Sam asks me.

I make a guess. "Fill it up?"

"Smart boy," he says. "County sees this hole and gets the same idea. Was my daddy's hole then. Thing was: the county man wasn't too crazy about paying some spook to use his landfill. Not in 1960, they weren't."

"So they bought him out?" I try another guess. Maybe something's clearer. I'm not sure what. Sam so rarely talks. About anything.

"What's this land worth? How much? Take a guess."

Since I don't have a clue, I just shrug.

"Land where your family's buried. Bought with blood and sweat. Tell me. How much?" He squares off in front of me, demanding an answer.

"There's . . . um . . . it's not for sale?"

"Damn right. Remember that." He goes back to his story. He's like in a trance. He kicks rocks and throws stones as he talks. Eventually we crouch down, squatting on our haunches like cavemen. You wouldn't want to sit down here.

"They offered plenty money. Some other land. Some good farm land down in the river valley. Daddy said 'no.' We held the title full and clear. That was that."

"They took the land?"

"Nothing's ever that simple, boy. Right here where we standing was a pile of soft powdered silt – so fine you couldn't get a footing. Daddy brought it in here figuring it might be worth something to somebody. One night a couple of little ones snuck in here to play." He says this and gives me one of his you-know-what-I-mean looks.

"They got in this mess just as a rain came. Like a cement it set up. Daddy found them the next morning half-dead from screaming and trying to get out. Right here it happened."

Sam rises and stretches out each long leg. One of his knees pops. I follow him back to the truck. He backs the truck out on Dorset, orders me out to padlock the gate.

"Those boys," I ask. "Were they all right?"

"Tired. Scared. Not half as scared as Daddy. Something inside him changed. He gave this hole away. The old fool just signed a paper and gave it away. Stuck them papers away in the back of some file like they was nothing. Just like that." Sam snaps his fingers. "Didn't say shit to me. To no one."

Sam laughed a bitter, full laugh. The sort of laugh the bad guys laugh in those James Bond films.

"The county was so grateful to him that they saved the hollow.

Suburban renewed us. Built the Washington Park Estates. God's Little Acre." He laughed his evil laugh some more.

"I don't see what's so funny."

"Don't you see, son? You and me, we the trash kings of Saint Louis County. This," he says, pulling into the driveway, "this is the house that trash built."

Sam stops laughing. He gives me a sour look. "I wouldn't of done it," he says. "And I sure wouldn't do it to you." He gets out of the truck, goes in the house, slams the door. I just sit there. In the truck. In the sun.

In my mind I jump out and go after him.

Come back here, I yell at him. Get to the punchline.

Is this about what is supposed to happen or what just happens anyway? About you or about me? Tell me what you want me to think, how I'm supposed to feel. Why'd you take me to your stupid dump? I don't half believe you anyway.

I get up enough courage to go in and ask questions. Which questions I don't know yet.

That fast he has changed into some of his good clothes. His silky white shirt and fancy brown blazer.

"I'll be out a little while," he says. "There's plenty of food, I think."

He lays a ten dollar bill on the cracked coffee table.

On the way out the door he stops and says to me, "You take what you get, you know?"

"No, I don't know."

Sam nods to indicate that that's okay, too.

*

From somewhere Miss Ida gets Artie some wheels: a 1975 Mustang, painted red. Well, it's not exactly red, it's faded to sort of a pink: Dentyne. That's what we call her, Dentyne. A beat-up old piece of car with multi-colored flecks and hunks of rust falling off it.

But she runs good. And Artie — who's turned sixteen already (seeing how he was left behind one year in first grade because he's so thick-headed) — is not the worst driver in the world as long as he refrains from showing off and can remember his left from his right and the brake pedal from the gas. Also, he will go almost anywhere you tell him to go, even though Miss Ida has specified school, the library, and the movies as the only legitimate stops. Sometimes Artie gets chicken. Then Todd and I have to twist his arm a little.

"You might as well take us where we want to go," I say. "We'll just tell your mom you went there anyway."

Artie pouts, whines, and drives on.

If you say the right thing, people will do whatever you want.

A while after Sam leaves, I hear rattling and honking.

Artie rolls down Dentyne's window. Todd shouts, "Let's go."

Sounds pretty good to me. I get the ten dollars, and we hit the road.

As soon as we clear Washington Park, Artie cranks up the Mustang as much as it will go. Not that fast. Much over forty and you get all of this smoking and shaking. This alarms poor Artie to no end. He has already developed some sort of paternal thing toward his piece of junk.

Artie snaps on his twenty-nine-cent fashion shades. He always wears them in the car, day or night. Betty Lou took him to some French love movie where the race car driver always wore dark glasses except when he was in bed with an actress with big boobs. That's just the way he described it. He wants Todd and me to wear sunglasses too so we will be a whole car full of cool dudes, but I tell him I'm not about to, and Todd says he'll have to get prescription ones, which are not listed anywhere that he knows of in the P.W.T. family budget. Pa P.W.T. gives Todd five dollars or so spending money a week. From what we hear it would not be a good idea to ask for more.

Truthfully it is only Artie who's got all this stuff: cash, clothes. A car, too, for that matter. There are no jobs in Washington Park except for a lawn to mow now and then. Sometimes Miss Ida hires us on to unload fresh stock at the store. Wherever we're going today, it had better be cheap.

Artie drives Dentyne out Colerain toward Chesterfield Mall. There, I spend part of the ten dollars on some greasy french fries, which make everyone sick. Hoping it will make us feel better, I make Artie spring for a large Orange Julius. It doesn't.

It's ninety-five degrees outside, so everyone is at the mall. The high school kids all sit by the center court fountain, because that's where you can see who else is here. They call that the meet market. The boys walk one way around the fountain and the girls walk the other. Unless you are already going with somebody. Then you parade around the upper level. The three of us sit there for a while and watch the show.

What do you know, here comes Connie Jo with this blond freshman chick. Even though it looks like they are headed in another direction, they veer off at the last minute and walk right in front of us — just close enough to make sure we see them. Connie's little girlfriend grabs Connie's arm and giggles.

Todd and I are pretending like they're not there, but then Artie says, real loud, "Hi Connie, hi Sue."

This Sue smiles and says, "Hi Arthur," which causes Connie Jo to look disgusted. She stares across the mall in the opposite direction.

Todd and I want to crawl beneath the fountain and die. I mean, one thing you don't do is actually talk to anyone. That's against the rules. But you could never explain that to Artie. He just barges right ahead.

"Having a good summer, Sue?" Artie goes on. I keep nudging him in his side.

"Guess what?" Sue says. "We're going to Disneyworld." Artie's eyes get big and she bubbles with excitement.

What, did she win the World Series of Bimbos? Her hair is all ratted out off the left side of her head. She stares at Artie as if he were a delicious chocolate bar. Artie looks faint. Or more faint than usual.

Connie Jo has the good sense to drag Sue away before the two of them can announce their engagement.

"See you in September," she calls as she's hauled away.

Artie's all smiles. "We have classes together," he says.

"Your mental retardation classes," I say.

"Learning disability," he says, all prim and proper. "And I ain't shame. People do the best they can. You're just jealous cause they spoke to me and not you."

Todd puts on his deepest drawl. "Son, her daddy'll have you and your learning disabilities strung up from the tallest tree in Ballwin."

"She's a nice friend," Artie says. "And everybody's not that way."

"Sure," I say.

How could someone like him get a girl to even think of talking to him? What's the deal on this? Artie's got some rich white gal talking to him, and the bimbos out here follow Todd around like kittens.

What am I, invisible?

"Look, look," Artie says. "It's Heather and Jennifer."

Todd suggests we get Elmer Fudd out of the mall before we all get lynched. We start to drive back up Lindberg. Artie spots Sue's car, so we have to go follow them around for a while. We go from the McDonald's to Steak and Shake to the Shell Station. Back around the mall. Every once in a while we pull up beside them. Sue and Artie wave moronic little waves at each other. Todd finds imaginative and unobvious ways of giving Connie Jo the finger. She doesn't see. She's hiding behind some Hollywood-sized dark glasses. I believe she is what is called mortified, which I am, too. I put my hands on both sides of my head like blinders.

"Can we just drive some place else, please," I say.

But that's the problem. There is nowhere else to go. It's hard to find creative ways to kill time.

*

Another Saturday Todd makes us stop at the main branch library on Lindberg. Todd carries loads of books these days. Books such as *The Fate of the Earth* and *Hunger in America*. Titles from the list Ohairy gave him for summer reading, books full of grim and awful information about the state of things. Some days Todd is impossible to talk to.

"Did you know," he asks, "that after a nuclear holocaust all that would survive would be grass and bugs?"

Another time: "What about nuclear winter? All of life would be dead. All of it."

That sort of thing.

Artie and I have to shut him up quick, because who wants to be depressed? I mean, we all have our own problems. For example, I was wondering how come it is that a person's life should turn out to be one way instead of a different way. I was really lying there on my bed thinking about that one. I mean, take for example all of those starving people over in the desert of Africa. If I had money for them or food for them, I'd give it to them in a second. I would, and I know that almost anyone else would, too. But, the point is, how is it that I got to be here in Washington Park, and they had to be there. What if it was just an accident? What if I woke up tomorrow and I was there, in the middle of nowhere, hungry? Instead of here with Sam? What would that be like? Would I think about McDonald's? Would I even know what that was? Or, you could wake up a soldier half-dead on a World War I battlefield. Or trapped under the rubble of a building in Pompeii. I think about that stuff sometimes until it starts to drive me crazy. Then I just stop. Sometimes it's best to think of nothing at all.

Todd persists, though. He reads in the car while we drive. You'd think he'd be carsick, especially with all this technical stuff he's reading — about chemical waste and nuclear reactors.

"I don't understand this," he whines, but he won't give up, ruining his already ruined eyes.

*

Every afternoon we go driving. We stop any place that might be free: any museum or park. We watch planes take off at the airport. We drive by all the rich people's houses in Ladue.

One stone house in Ladue has three or four stories, must have a hundred and fifty rooms. The swimming pool could hold two crackerboxes.

"Look at these joints," I say. I just can't imagine having so much dough. "Who lives here? Where do they get the money?"

"From poor people," Todd says. "People like you and me." I feel one of his new lectures coming on. Todd goes on and on as to how he read in one of his books how rich people get money by making poor people work for them. He says there have to be poor people because there are rich people. He says a lot of other crap, too, and he says it in this real smug way — as if he knew what he was talking about.

"It doesn't sound fair to me," I say. "If it's true."

"Oh, it's true, all right. And, it's not fair to you or to anyone else, either."

Artie says, "Prob'ly some of them get the money from their parents. Nothing wrong with that."

"Where do you think their parents got it, bonehead." I say. I say this because Todd is all of the sudden so sincere, so convincing. So much so, I feel like I should be on his side.

I add, "The point is they got it and we don't. Maybe not ever." I stare up the lawns at all these joints and think about the life me and Sam could have there. We'd have cooks and maids for sure, I know that much.

"You don't have to be so mean," Artie whines. He drives us by a famous architect's house, by a house with a stable, by a five car garage.

"Do you think having all this stuff is worth it?" I ask.

"Worth what?" Todd asks. "The suffering of others? The guilt?"

"Worth whatever it costs. However they get it."

Todd thinks for a while. "All I know is it is worth doing whatever you have to do to make things more fair in the world."

"You'll never change the world." I say.

"But I'll try. What about you?"

*

One day there's Todd in the back seat, big tears rolling down his freckled cheeks. Artie pulls over in the Target parking lot.

"So what are we going to do?" Todd wants to know. "We have to do something. How can they do this? How can they leave it like this for us?" He's seething.

"Do about what?" I ask.

"About any of it. We're part of this shit, and we got to do something." He shouts.

"No reason to get upset," I say. "Maybe there's nothing we can do."

"That's not good enough for me," he answers.

*

This is how we spend the whole summer I am fifteen. Artie driving, cool and smug, Todd getting angrier and more frightened by the day. Me just watching. Almost dead from boredom. Nothing ever happens to me.

Todd sees stuff going down all around us—poisoned air, nuclear bombs, all kinds of stuff. Some of it too awful to imagine. For some reason I cannot get excited about it. All that happens somewhere else, to someone else. Sometimes I think I don't have much of a life at all.

Oh, poor Marshall, you'd say. But that's not what I mean at all. What I'm talking about is how stuff can go on all around you and you don't know about it at all. And when you find out about it, you just feel used and stupid.

Take Sam and Betty Lou Warner, for instance.

All summer long.

Right under our noses.

You'd think I didn't know my father at all.

7

WHAT YOUR PARENTS do is none of your business. Or maybe that should be a question.

I guess to their credit Big Sam and Betty Lou Warner were discreet. No one — meaning me — suspected anything.

Paying attention I'd have found clues at every turn. All of the time when Sam would be gone, and then I'd hear that Betty had been gone, too. Once or twice I'd joked that something was up, and I remember feeling just a little uncomfortable, since you just don't joke about something like this when it involves your parent. I mean what if it were true? But, then, Sam's a good ten years older than Betty, and what would he possibly want with someone like her anyway. She must know some tricks or something. Betty has a reputation, kind of a bad one. She always had a lot of different dudes around — lots that Artie himself doesn't even know. When these dudes show up, Artie either comes up to my house, or stays up at Miss Ida's. The one time I asked about them he told me to mind my own damn business. That's how close he is to Betty. I know better than to meddle in family business anyway.

But, what about when his family business becomes my family business?

Which brings us to what ought probably to have been a major indication something was up. In July we decided we were going to the Cards game and we decided to sit in the bleachers because it's cheap, and also because on a hot day in the bleachers when the niggers and the honkies get tanked up on Busch, out there in the sun anything's likely to happen. Big Sam himself says this, and the day we were there, in fact, this big black dude stands up and hollers at Ozzie that they ought to send his black butt back to the farm, at which point this redneck just up from Kentucky stands up and hollers that niggers never could hit worth a shit, at which point punches were thrown, and beer and all kinds of stuff starts flying. Us boys hustle up to the concession stands because here is a major race riot in progress and we want a place we can see the whole thing. The riot fizzled out when folks got tired of shoving around in all that heat, and also because there was a double play on the field.

"That Busch got em," as Big Sam would say.

The three of us just stood there and laughed our asses off.

On the way home we get off the highway on Old Olive Street and that crummy Dentyne gets a flat. Well, that happens a lot. We're experts at fixing them fast.

Then here comes the weird part: Sam says to me, "I hear you fellas had a little excitement."

"Sir?"

"Little business with a flat tire?"

And I quick wonder how he knew about that, since, generally speaking, flat tires don't make the evening news. But Sam's not the sort of person you ask how he knows anything.

I ask Artie if he mentioned the flat tire to anyone. He says no.

"Not even Betty?" I ask him, knowing full well that he tells Betty everything. Even when his bowels move.

"Well, yes," he says all sheepish. I tell him that Big Sam also knew, but once again real life gets written off as coincidence. We figured they'd run into each other at the gas station.

Mostly it was lack of imagination that blinded us.

*

Then late in July there was this major distraction. A letter from Rose. It said:

Marshall,

Wish there was a way to make you read this. Couldn't even if I was there with you, could I? You know I'd try. I'll write anyway. I feel like I need to.

You're about the only person I can think of to write to. I made lists and lists of all the folks I know. Your name came up on the top of every one. Figure it must mean something. Guess I got some things to tell you.

Kinda funny, ain't it. You and me about as angry at each other as two people can be. I'm trying to work it all out. Hope you are, too.

So I've landed out here in Vegas. Bet everybody knew that but you. Ever body protects little Marshall.

Course, first thing I learn is, you can run but you can't hide. From your people, that is.

First night I'm here I have a dream and it's my mama. Like a ghost. Looking just like the last time I seen her alive.

"What you think you doing, girl?" she says to me. "Running off like this."

So I tell her I need some time to myself. And she tells me I better grow up. Here's the facts: I'm thirty four, been married since eighteen. When was my time to grow up? Married half my life and you and Sam bout the only folks I know in the whole world.

So busy being a good girl. Doing what everybody says. Mama and daddy. Nuns at school. Sam. You.

So here I up and done something on my own. I did what they do in the movies, what they tell you to do in the women's lib books: I got up and got out. It's the hardest thing I probably ever will do. Maybe the only thing.

And even the ghosts don't leave you alone.

The only thing I done except have a baby. You were a cute baby. A baby needs you all the time. Gives you a reason to be. And then one day you turned into Marshall. And what then?

What is it Marshall wants from me now?

I looked up one day and found myself sitting in some crackerbox in Washington Park, all day long, with not a damn thing to do. That's what Sam wanted, see. Someone sitting up waiting for him to get home. And don't think of trying to do something like go to school or get a job. You just sit and be looking fine. Like you was a doll or a paper cut out.

To hell with that. There I was getting crazier than a circus monkey. Talking back to Big Bird on Sesame Street.

You knew I was crazy, no? You acted like you did.

When you were a little boy I'd wait for you to come home and tell me about your big day at school. We'd color and draw together. That and Days of Our Lives was about the high point of my day.

Then all of a sudden one day Marshall's an overgrown moose, and it was as if to you I had disappeared. So I decided to hell with that little nigger. I read my books, did my nails, and watched TV. In the back of my mind I thought I ought to get a skillet and bash your black brains in. Here you get to go out in the world and be somebody, and I'm locked in like some damn prisoner. I'd see the butcher knife and I'd dig my nails into my palms and pray for God to help me. Such a thin line between love and hate.

I want you to remember it's me I'm talking about here. I saved my money and left. Ain't nothing to be proud of, I know. Sometimes you gotta save your own self.

More later,

Love mother

*

Imagine getting a letter like that. From anyone, but from your mother? I fold it up and drop it between a random page of the Ci-Cz World Book encyclopedia. There is almost never a reason to look there.

For days I walk by the bookshelf and I see that book. I see it even when I'm in the other room doing the dishes, when I'm lying back on my bed staring at the ceiling. I see that book and think about the letter inside. The letter I can't read again. The one I oughtn't have read at all.

I think about people like Rose: the quitters and cheaters of the world. I wonder should they be hated or just pitied.

The game wasn't going in her favor. Things as bad as they could be. So she just walks away. Which is the same as giving up, right?

Still, I wished her well, and I meant it.

Remember: looking back is no fair, always against the rules — even in the Bible.

I see that book. Ci-Cz. In my mind only I tear that letter into a million billion pieces. In the desert Rose turns into a pillar of salt.

*

So I have more on my mind than where Big Sam parks his truck at night. To tell the truth I loved not having him around, loved having the house to myself. We would drive around all night long, all summer. The boys and I never got caught. When Sam came in — if Sam

71

came in—he would be half asleep or half drunk. He's a big boy. He put himself to bed.

On August fifteenth we'd stopped for gas at the Fina station on North Lindberg. The station up along that strip by the airport where there are only airline offices, motels, and off-brand rent-a-car places. Artie was pumping the gas and Todd and I were splitting a Pepsi. This is about 8:30, and as we're getting in the car Todd says, "Marsh, ain't that your old man's truck over there?"

He points me where I see a brown Dodge over by the office of the Air View Motel.

"Same kind, sure," I say.

Artie says, "Looks like Big Sam's got himself a little something on the side."

"Right, muthafucker," I say. "With your mom."

"Watch that stuff," he says, and we all chase each other around the Mustang and spray each other with shook-up Pepsi foam.

As we go to pull out on Lindberg, Todd says, "Holy shit."

There's Sam, big as life, coming out of the motel office with his arm around Betty Lou. Right there for the whole world to see.

Artie's frozen at the wheel for what seems like hours while we watch the two of them over there in the evening's fading light. Then, with a start, Artie floors the gas pedal like he means for us to take off and fly over there. We are saved only because Todd thinks quickly enough to turn the wheel. We spin back into the gas station, barely avoiding three cars and an eighteen wheeler.

"You're not gonna get me killed, asshole," Todd yells. Then he wants to know why I'm ducked down in the back seat.

"They'll see us," I say.

"We're the last thing they're looking to see," Todd sniggers.

"Shut up," says Artie. The wheel is clutched tightly in his fists and his eyes are full of water.

"Calm down," says Todd. "Just drive home. Pretend it never happened."

Miraculously Artie does drive, and for a long time it is quiet—Artie driving like a robot chauffeur.

Artie pulls the car in behind Miss Ida's. I imagine he'll stay there now.

As long as nobody's talking I figure I'll go on home. So I say good night. I start walking down the hill.

Someone jumps me from behind, knocks me to the ground. It is Artie, sobbing and whimpering, trying to make contact with his fists. But he is weak and spindly, and I'm the overgrown moose here. Before he can do any damage I roll him over and start to pulverize him.

"Stop it." This is Todd hollering. He grabs me around the waist to pull me off. He can barely hold me.

I get up, brush off and start for home again, but here comes Artie for more. I shove him back. "I'm gonna whoop your ass, nigger," I say. I knock him down, at which point Todd steps between us.

"Enough," he orders.

I'm ready to really lay into him, but Todd's got him restrained. Artie's sobbing and gasping for breath.

"For chrissakes, Marshall, just go home," Todd says.

I give them my best Sam Finney tough guy look and walk off real slow.

*

Sam drifts in sometime the next morning. He is as smug as ever, and why wouldn't he be?

I let myself get good and stewed about the whole mess.

"I saw you yesterday," I say at dinner.

He raises an open-handed palm as if to say "so what?"

"We went to the gas station. Up by the airport." I leave it at that.

Sam scratches his head for a little while. "Don't play games with me, boy," he says.

"You shouldn't have . . ."

"Best not on your life ever tell me what I should and shouldn't do."

I wait a while and say, "Well, anyway. Poor Artie. You know how he is about his sister."

"His mama," he says. And then he says, "That's what I said, and get that look off your face. Everybody knows that Betty Lou's that boy's mama."

Who is everybody? How do they find this stuff out? Sam wasn't taking any questions.

"This is horrible." I say. "I always thought Miss Ida . . ."

"You don't know much, do you," Big Sam says. He looks at me with a real superior look. He's even got a smile on his face.

"You ain't got a problem with this, do you?" he asks.

"No. It's just that . . . people shouldn't . . . it doesn't seem right."

"You judge people, boy. Too harsh. You got that from your mama. Rose, she never could look past nothing. That's wrong. You got to learn to look past people's fault. Everybody makes mistakes. You got to learn to forgive. Now, I may not be a Christian man, but I know one thing Jesus was set on. It's just part of being a man. Forgive and get on with life."

I am not like her. Not at all. And:

"Well, if everybody is so forgiving, then why the big secret."

"No secret," Sam says. "It's just not anybody's business. What business is it of yours who that boy's mama is? It don't change the way you feel about him. I hope you're not that bad."

"No, sir," I say.

"You about a lie," Sam says. He chuckles. "I've got something to take care of." He grabbed the truck keys and left.

*

Who knows what Big Sam said to Betty. Whatever: that was pretty much the end of the Sam and Betty Lou thing.

Artie, Betty Lou, and Miss Ida: three people I'd known almost my whole life. And then you find out something like this. What I know now is that it's not what happens that gets you, it's the way you find out what happens. Finding out, you wonder if there is something about people that you just can't see, if everyone you know has got some terrible secret hidden away. In a way Sam is right — it does change the way you feel, but not just about the one with the secret. It makes me wonder about everyone.

*

The aftermath:

As for Sam, for a while he's around most evenings. He goes into some kind of state, though, and he's drunk a lot of the time on Budweiser or cheap wine. The shopping is again left to me, as is everything else around the house.

Artie stays up at the store, and Todd stays across the tracks.

Just before school starts up I stop in at Miss Ida's for a few groceries. Betty Lou is behind the counter.

"Marshall, my man," she says. She gives me a big hug. I don't want to hug her, but she looks like she needs one: her eyes look sad and watery. She looks lost.

"Mama," she hollers, "look who's here."

When Miss Ida comes out, Betty Lou throws a big pink satchel over her shoulder. She tells me to come see her sometime and leaves.

"My poor baby," Miss Ida says behind her. "Artie still won't have nothing to do with her."

She takes my list and starts packing: cereal, chocolate syrup, canned fish.

"Some things just ruin everything, don't they?"

"It seems that way," I say to her.

"Go upstairs and see your friend," she says to me.

"I don't know . . ."

"Go ahead. He's been moping up there for days."

Artie lies up on the couch watching MTV. His skin is ashy-gray, either from the light or from being locked away so long.

"Hey," I say.

But he just goes to his room and slams the door.

*

I keep saying what I learned—from this or that. It's hard not to. When I saw Artie laying up there in the store, and he walked away from me the way he did, sure I felt sad for him, but also there was a strange feeling—a feeling just as if I had my foot on the back of his neck.

Miss Ida says some things ruin everything.

Power + hormones—and the world blows up.

All of these people's lives touched and changed. Maybe if Sam had kept his dick in his pants and maybe if Betty weren't so ready and willing . . .

Is it that some of them feel as lonely as I sometimes do? I know I don't know what the chemistry is or how it works. If chemistry is even what it is in the first place. I know you have to worry about all these emotions. Things can get out of control, and then you're lost.

I believe it, too. I believe the world could blow up. Because of a Yeats poem.

Or a good piece of fried chicken.

8

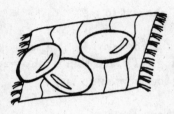 THE FIRST DAY of school there is a junior class meeting. Todd and I go together. Artie doesn't show up at the bus stop, but I see his car parked on the lot in front of the school. We sit on an aisle real conspicuous so he can see us. He goes up front and sits alone.

Already there is going to be talk: damn these Pinheads — if a booger fell out of your nose at ten it would be all over school by lunch. I want to stand up and shout "it's just a friendly spat," but then maybe your dad doing it with your friend's mom might be more than a friendly spat.

Todd lies back real low in his chair and folds his arms on his chest. He's scoping the two hundred or so pinheads. He's clearly got something on his mind. With him, you can never be too sure what it might be.

Retiring queen Connie Jo calls the meeting to order. There are wolf whistles and howls all around in appreciation of the little walk to which Connie Jo treats us on the way to the podium. She clicks her heels and waves her ass in such a way that her flowery skirt sways back and forth in wide swoops. She blushes with shame, but she's not shame at all. She is wearing entirely too many clothes for September second, but I guess she has a lot of new ones to show off quick before they go out of style.

"Hey everybody," she chirps, "I hope you all had a super summer. I know I did." Connie Jo goes on to say how she is looking forward to a super year, and then goes on to remind us of what a super year we had last year, and then to remind us of all of the super things she'd planned and done for us, and then on to introduce Buzz — her "coworker" — without whom . . . blasé, blasé, and so on and so forth. The usual Miss America retirement speech.

Next to me Todd mumbles "dumb bitch" and other such things, and every few minutes Artie turns around, I guess checking to see if it is in fact us and if we are indeed still here.

"And now juniors," enthuses Connie Jo, "I have an exciting announcement."

A few people yell "go for it" and "whip it out."

"As you know Mr. Anderson, the junior class advisor, is no longer with us."

A loud, insincere moan fills the air.

"But I'm pleased to announce we have a replacement, and let me introduce our new advisor, Miss O'Hare."

The audience applauds wildly for Miss O'Hare who comes from backstage. Todd sits right up like a rocket in his chair. His applause is the loudest.

O'Hare has on her no nonsense business suit — the dark blue one with the white blouse. She nods, receiving the applause cordially enough, and then puts on her glasses and gets right down to the point.

"Thank you for that. I, too, hope you've had a good summer, but school has started which means it's time to get our minds to the tasks at hand." She reads this from a notecard. So well does she control her voice and her eyes, the Pinheads give her full attention. Or as full as it gets around here.

"I asked our assistant principal, Mr. Shannon, for permission to form an issues discussion group. Mr. Shannon asked me to take on the role of junior class sponsor. He reminded me of all the exciting events ahead of us: the powder-puff football game, homecoming, winter fun daze, and, of course, prom. I remember my own junior class experiences.

"The week of my prom four young people — some not much older than you are now — were shot to death on the campus of Kent State University in Ohio. Our party went on as planned and a great time was had by all."

At this Todd smiles broadly and rubs his hands together. The Pinheads are in various stages of confusion. Connie Jo, sitting on stage, is genuinely alarmed — you can tell this because she looks as if she were looking for someone to come up there and help her. Connie's a trooper, though, and she smiles right through it. Ohairy goes on:

"Well, the war's over. Ten years now, and there aren't National Guard troops on campuses with guns at the ready. At least I hope not. Today, instead, we have uncontrolled nuclear proliferation, world hunger, and global injustice to face."

Todd shakes a fist and says "yes!" real loud. Someone up front boos.

"Don't worry, I'm almost done," she says pointedly. Connie Jo clenches her fists. "I want to wish you a *super* year: best of luck on your little dances and things. You certainly don't need my help for them, and truthfully they interest me about this much." Miss O'Hare indicates a small distance between her thumb and forefinger.

Todd alone applauds; Ohairy acknowledges him with smiling eyes.

"As always I'm available for serious discussions. Please don't waste my valuable time on color schemes."

O'Hare interrupts a smattering of applause. It is led by the now standing Todd. She finishes with, "One more thing: serious candidates and issues for class elections, okay? You are dismissed to your homerooms."

The Pinheads stagger out mumbling and whispering to each other. Artie wanders away in the herd.

"What a woman," Todd says to me. He is still on cloud nine.

"Sort of a downer for the first day of school," I say to him.

"You ain't seen nothing yet," he says. "We're gonna set this fucker on its ear."

*

Late in September Todd announces his intention of running for class president. Imagine: the nerve of a poor kid from the wrong side of even the wrong side of the tracks . . . I tell him this, too. Tell him that Pinheads don't vote white trash into elected office. That doesn't stop him. We go to tell Miss O'Hare, who says, "Perfect."

"We've got to plan carefully if this is going to work." She starts sketching in a note pad, looking at Todd. Sometimes she stares at him, hard, as if she were trying to memorize his face. He stares right back at her, boldly, in a way I never would. In a way he wouldn't have too long ago himself. He's smiling and I can see the wheels in her head turning. She looks at Todd as if he were some kind of a prize, or a side of beef, and she a hungry lion.

I'm in on the first stages of the campaign, because, for a while, Todd plays like he is still too shy to go to her office alone. That isn't true, and it isn't too long before he's practically sitting on her lap, drinking in her every word. It's embarrassing, especially when she tells him what he thinks and why he thinks it and what's the best way to get himself elected.

This is all on the sly, too, because in public O'Hare pretends to be neutral. Which is what she's supposed to be.

One Monday morning in October, Todd shows up at the bus stop, and there's something different about him, I can tell, though I can't quite tell what it is.

"Well," he says, smiling.

"Did you get new glasses?" I guess.

"Kathy took me to the city last weekend. That's where we found these clothes. Great, huh?"

"Kathy?" I say. He grins even bigger.

"She says it's okay to call her that. What do you think? Really." He models the new look.

"Kathy? She bought you clothes?"

"Cheap stuff. From a second-hand place in Soulard. I spent some of my own money. I bought her a rose." He rocks on his heels and gives me this raised eyebrow look.

"You're in way over your head here." I tell him.

"I'm teasing," he laughs. "It's nothing like that. Really. She's a . . . just really a good person. She listens to me. Like a good friend."

"I listen. I'm a good friend." I say this with mock-hurt in my voice.

"You're ugly and you wear the same socks for a whole week."

This is true.

"I see your point," I say.

The change in appearance takes me a while to see. You take your friends for granted that way. Sometimes you hardly see them at all. But when I do look I notice that Todd is definitely a new Todd. She'd had his hair cut just a few inches shorter, and layered in such a way that it swept back naturally to where he tucked it behind his ears.

On the clothes she'd done something trickier. She'd replaced the army jacket with an old suit vest and suspenders over a dress shirt. Very impressive, even with the jeans.

The overall impression: Wash U — he looked like a lot of those guys down at Washington University. It is enough to make the Pinheads, most of whom never before gave him the time of day, take notice.

*

By the time Todd and O'Hare choose a campaign theme, my presence is long past necessary, so I can't say what happened. I bet they fought like a couple of mad hens, with Todd heavily favoring "NO NUKES" and O'Hare pushing "U.S. OUT OF CENTRAL AMERICA."

"I don't see why she's so stubborn about a campaign slogan," Todd says to me. "This is our chance to really get my issue out there."

His issue.

I tell him that she probably has in mind what was best for winning the election.

He says neither of them are expecting any trouble with that.

Todd wins the argument. They go with "NO NUKES." The election is set for national election day in November.

*

Meanwhile, Sam comes home every night, or is careful to let me know why not.

No. Sam comes home. Drunk mostly. I don't know how he gets to the landfill every day. Or if he does. I imagine him asleep in the truck, fallen over in a chair in the recycling shed. I imagine him driving around doing nothing.

He takes up the shopping again, but I have to stop in at Miss Ida's for real food, he's so bad at it. Around the time the leaves are falling, this is what I unpack from his shopping bag: four green apples, one turkey pot pie, two packages of double fudge cake mix, a one and a half pound bag of Doritos. And, of course, two six packs of Bud.

"There's no food in here," I yell.

Sam clumps into the kitchen, slowly, as if there is lead in his body. "No, I suppose not," he says. He takes a beer and goes back to the TV.

One afternoon Todd and I hitch a ride up to the mall to get the stuff for the campaign posters. We catch a Bi-State bus home, and Todd stops by my house to work on posters. He says it'll at least be quiet here, but I bet there's not been a favorable reaction to radical politics down in P.W.T. land. More and more Todd's been saying he can't talk to them down there. This is after never saying a word about them ever.

I open the front door and go turn on the TV. Todd says something about having to "drain the snake."

80

"Marshall," he says. "Come back here."

There on the bathroom floor, Sam lies with his face in a pool of vomit. He moans, so it is clear he's not dead.

I don't know what to do. I say "I'm sorry" to Todd. Todd looks at me annoyed. I shake Sam and ask him to get up.

Sam slurs out my name.

"Come on," Todd says. "You can't talk to them when they're like this. Grab under his arm there. I've got this side."

I follow along as directed.

"Don't be a pussy. You're gonna get puke on you. It washes off." Todd apparently knows. The vomit smells sour, of beer and rot.

We hoist him up. Todd says, "We'll have to drag him a little. He's a heavy dude."

By and by we are able to haul Sam to his room and drop him on his bed. He grunts and groans. He says my mother's name. He is too far out of it to do much else.

I wet a washcloth and take it in to him. As I wipe around his face he moves his head around as if the rag hurts him.

"Stop, Marshall," he moans. He brings a swollen hand up to still the rag. He mumbles something else and I fight down the urge to scream my hatred.

Back in the bathroom Todd is on his hands and knees wiping up the mess with a roll of paper towels.

"You don't have to do that," I tell him.

"It's okay," he says. He looks at me with a kind smile. "We get a lot of this down our way."

"We don't get a lot of it here," I turn my back to him.

Later Todd joins me in the kitchen where I've started tracing giant globes on the posterboards. Anything to get my mind off of Sam.

"It could be a lot worse for you," Todd says.

Just then I don't see quite how.

*

Big Sam doesn't look me in the eye for a week. He ducks in and out like a criminal on the lam. Sometimes stumbling and staggering; other times overcorrecting each step

I cook what I can — what Miss Ida and Betty credit us. Money's been short and Sam's not been paying the tab.

The first cold day, early November, I heat up some beef stew and Sam sits down to eat it. I begrudge him every drop of it.

"I'll try. It'll be better," he says. "It's just so hard, you understand. Different than I planned."

I glare at him. The steam rises between us from the canned stew. "What's hard?" I ask. "Tell me."

He picks up his soup bowl and empties it in one gulp. He gets up and walks by me, rubbing his hand through my hair.

My whole body quivers.

*

Each candidate is limited to ten posters. Connie Jo Hartberger, running on the school spirit ticket, makes full use of the limited space. All of her posters scream out from the walls, proclaiming FUN and GOOD TIMES with glitter, ribbons, and fluorescent paints.

Todd's ten posters are identical. A bright blue map of the world with "NO NUKES" lettered across diagonally in red stenciled letters. Written across the bottom in green letters "Sponsored by the Todd Lawrence for junior class president campaign."

I tell Todd these posters are completely the wrong idea. Who around here cares about this stuff? They think he wants them to give up their microwaves.

Which is just the point, he answers.

*

Sam comes up behind me where I am sitting on the couch watching MTV. He puts his hands on my shoulders.

"I guess this is the way it's gonna be from now on. I guess I'm gonna have to accept that."

He kneads my shoulders. He leans into me with all his weight. Madonna spins around on the floor.

"I kept waiting. I kept hoping. But I gotta get on with my life now."

I hear him walk away down the hall and close the door to his room. I turn up the TV a little louder.

*

The class assembly:
Connie Jo – transformed into Marilyn Monroe – is borne on a flower-

laden platter into the auditorium by a gang of tuxedoed football players, one waving a fan at her – up her dress – which she coyly smoothes down. All the while she's blowing kisses and smacking her cherry red lips.

A nice illusion but about fifty pounds too much of it. A few times the jocks almost spill poor Marilyn to the waiting wolves below.

Miss H. breathes a heartfelt rendition of "Connie is Your School's Best Friend."

"A vote for a blond who is quite sentimental . . ."

She floors them. A Pinhead ovation.

Then it is Todd's turn. He comes out alone. He has added a tie to the simple jeans, vest combo. His speech is written on one three by five card.

"Students and staff. Throughout the world today thousands of pounds of nuclear waste await proper storage and burial. The amount increases every day. It will remain harmful for hundreds of centuries. Every year the number of countries with nuclear potential increases, and with it grows the potential of nuclear war and of accidental detonation. Or of a small scale nuclear confrontation that would poison the globe. More and more scientists and physicians recognize the necessity for gaining control of the nuclear problem before it leads to our final annihilation. When elected class president I will bring these issues and others before you for intelligent debate. Thank you."

He smiles in a way that is both sincere, serious, and also highlights his dimples.

Afterwards Todd asks me how he did. It's clear he's pleased. I tell him the applause for him was less than for Marilyn.

"I don't think many of them really vote, do you?" he asks me.

How should I know?

"By the way," he says, "I have here in my hand the terms of surrender."

Before I can protest, he flips over and reads from the same three-by-five card he'd used for the speech.

"Artie says he's willing to consider making up if you agree to allow him to say as many mean and rude things to you as he wants to for up to and not to exceed five minutes. With, of course, no rebuttal and no repercussions."

"That's stupid." I say.

"It's the best I could do. Is it a deal?"

Why not?

Then it's election day.

I should have known.

I did know.

There's Miss O'Hare wearing an American flag on her lapel. There's Todd all smiles.

I bet less than one hundred votes are cast. After the car crack from Todd, I, myself, mark a ballot for Connie Jo. It won't make a bit of difference.

Miss O'Hare, very business-like, crosses the podium at the assembly to read the results. The two candidates flank her. Connie Jo has her chest thrust out so it appears her breasts will pop out of that sweater at any moment. She keeps giving these looks to Todd that are either gloating, flirting, or maybe both. As for Todd, he looks as if he'd be happy to spit on everyone in the room. The same look O'Hare has.

"Lawrence 125, Hartberger 87. Congratulations, Todd."

There is a smattering of applause. The Pinheads get up and leave. No one really cares about these class elections anyway. Todd knew that all along, and Ohairy knew that, too. Connie Jo stands there open-mouthed, red in the face, teary. O'hare gives her a "I-dare-you-to-call-me-a-liar" look. Connie Jo walks away. I guess she will have to settle for prom queen this year.

I don't know what to say to Todd on the bus.

"Congratulations" is the best I can do.

He just shrugs, says a quiet "Thanks." And then, "You do what you have to do."

"I'm not quite sure what you're sayin," I say to him.

"I'm not sure what *you're* saying."

"Did you cheat? You can tell me. I won't say anything."

"Is that what you think?" he asks with a sneer.

"It's true, isn't it?"

He just laughs at me.

"We won," he says. "That's all that matters."

I think about it a minute. "That's not quite all there is to it," I say. "You know, if you did, you won't get away with it."

"If I did cheat — and I'm not saying I did — I think I already did get away with it." Todd says. He shakes his head and laughs some more.

"But you're just full of shit if you think I didn't win fair and square."

"I don't." I tell him, "You're pretty cool now. But what if it were just you. No Ohairy. Just you."

"It is me," he says. "Just me. Don't ever forget that."

I tell him I won't.

*

Which leaves the truce. Todd arranges for Artie to come to my house after school.

"Does everybody understand the rules?" he asks.

I, restricted from speaking, only nod.

Todd indicates for Artie to begin. He eyes me for a long time with an expression that goes from mean, to quizzical, and back again to mean. Finally he says, "Forget it."

"That's it?" I ask, but Todd reminds me that Artie's time isn't up.

"All I want is, I just don't want, I . . . don't like it when people think I'm dumb," Artie says. "It hurts when people treat you that way."

I feel like dirt.

Todd orders me to shake Artie's hand.

Right then, Sam, unexpectedly early, comes in from the landfill. I have no idea how Artie'll react.

Sam merely waltzes in, grin stretched from ear to ear, eyes all aglow.

"Men!" he cheers, and then gives us each a pat on the head on the way to his room. Artie flinches and Todd's mouth drops open.

Behind Sam's back I point at him and shake my head. I roll my eyes. Artie nods in agreement and I give high five.

Artie: as soft as a newborn baby. I'm sure I'll know him the rest of my life, so I guess I better learn to respect him.

But he's weak. Much too weak.

Weakness is just not to be tolerated.

9

THE FIRST SNOW in early December is a snow almost like rain. In the morning Artie won't drive: too chicken. So it's back to the school buses for us. It is still snowing late in the day. The antique bus we ride groans and grinds on the icy streets, and the back end waves like a fishtail. To be safe, Artie and Todd and I get off way back on Colerain Road, by the 7-Eleven, and we walk the mile in to Washington Park. There's no saying we wouldn't have rolled off into a ravine or slid into a semi on a day like this.

The snow is gloppy thick and the three of us roll around and pelt each other with mushy wads of it, acting like we are the Pinheads back at Eisenhower, or like we are puppies out in our first snow. I catch Todd in his ruddy nose with an ice ball, and just when I am sure he'll start to bleeding or something, he picks up a huge slab of snow that is stuck together with ice and is enough to smother both Artie and me. He mushes it right in our faces. Icicles drip from his stringy red hair and in Artie's and my naps the snow looks like cotton balls and lint. We hoot and holler as the trucks spray us with charcoal slush.

*

The flag is up on the mailbox out by the curb. I reach in to see what's new besides bills. What do I find but a postcard from Rose. On a day like this here's a picture of palm trees and swimming pools sparkling in the sun. On the back it says:

86

Hi Marshall:

Life do be complicated. But things are changing over, I know. Still haven't won a pot. But as long as I got a quarter in my pocket . . .

Always,
Ma

I drop it and shake my head.

Of course, there is no sign of Big Sam, which is just as well because I don't need to be listening on a day like this to a lecture about being soaking wet and out in the cold like a fool. Not that one could get such a lecture around here. I crank up the TV and peel off the wet clothes. They get dumped in a corner for when I'll do the laundry. I put on a sweater and some overalls, and fire up the thermostat another ten degrees.

There isn't too much around for supper. That's been typical lately. Like I'm supposed to live on the bizarre stuff Sam picks up when he happens by Miss Ida's. Today in the cupboard are a can of kipper snacks and two boxes of Captain Crunch – my favorite foods, canned fish and sugar.

I make a big pot of macaroni and then shave off the mold from an ancient chunk of cheddar cheese and throw the chopped up cheese in the pot along with some margarine and milk. For spite, I pepper it up real good – more than I like it myself – so that should old Sam drag himself in from another night of "just stepping out for a few minutes" and have stomach and taste buds left, he'd burn his ornery tongue real good. Serve him right. I shovel the biggest of the noodles out on a paper plate and wolf them down with some extra sugary raspberry Kool-aid.

Outside it's still snowing. The huge heavy flakes are sticking together now. They fall in chunks that look like they ought to make a splat when they land. I do trigonometry homework and fall asleep in front of a Christmas special – some old white guy singing carols up in the mountains. Big Sam wakes me when he blows in the door like Jack Frost himself. He's blustering and shaking like a big yard dog.

"It's something else out there," he says. As if there were someone else in the room who didn't already know, or who cared more than me. He sits – more reclines – back in one of the kitchen chairs, his body leaned like a plank against the wall. He slowly unlaces his workboots by dragging first one foot up his leg and then another, looking for all the world as if he'd just walked from the North Pole, waiting for me to ask him where he's been.

Out of habit I get up and move the boots to the tub where they can drain—not needing to, in addition to whatever else, mop up after him, too. The leather is soaked clean through.

I can't smell that he's been drinking tonight, even though his eyes are veined red. He is able to get the boots unlaced on his own, so he must be sober. I come back in and he is curled over the table with his face in his hands rubbing his head that is beady with water.

"I'm beat," he says. "I musta pushed out every stuck car in Washington Park. Down across the tracks, too."

"I made some food if you want it," I say. I feel a little shamed for what I've done to it. And I know he must be tired because he just shakes his head and hauls himself up and I hear him crash on his big empty bed.

*

When the phone rings I wake up startled; no one ever calls here in the middle of the night. I know I'd better get it because there's no way that Big Sam is gonna get himself up.

"Put Sam on," says this twangy voice that I recognize as Arnie Nelson, Sam's supervisor from the county. I can hear the joy he is having at waking us.

"He's sleeping," I say.

"Tell you what: you tell him he best be gettin himself up. We got a mess out there with that snow. The Park needs to be plowed. Down to the river bottom, too. Before rush hour." He hangs up.

The bastard.

It is three o'clock in the morning. Waking Big Sam at any hour is like going into the bear's den. But to get him up for plowing . . .

"Daddy." I lean in gingerly and shake his big frame. You got to be careful when you wake him in case he decides to lash out.

"Rose," he mumbles.

"Hey! Daddy!" I call a little louder, shake a little harder.

"Gu wu," he growls into a pillow.

"Come on, Daddy. Mr. Nelson says you gotta get the streets plowed. Let's go."

He sits up quick like he has been shocked; sits rubbing his eyes like a little boy would. "M'late for work again." He says that the way he usually does when I wake him from oversleeping.

"No. It's snowing. You have to plow. Right now."

"Sheeit," he says. He rolls back, spread-eagle.

"Dad?"

"Well. I guess that settles it — no more county work for me. There's no way."

"What's settled? I don't get it." He rolls over: he isn't going anywhere.

"Ain't no way I can do all that. I might as well let it go. Get some rest rather than even waste the time." He pulls up the covers to show he means it.

"You usually do it," I am coaxing him, but it sounds more like I am cursing him. Who'd expect he was this lazy?

"Look here: when does it snow this much? Huh?"

He had a point: hardly ever.

"And old Porter usually helps me — he's too sick. So that's that."

Which is when I think fast: "Artie and Todd and me." I don't see his reaction because I'm busy figuring how I'll manage waking those two. "Hurry and we can make it."

Big Sam hesitates and then gets himself going. Even if he hates plowing, he knows and I know we need the money.

How could you live like Sam — with no planning ahead, never expecting the worst, which people like me figure'll happen sooner or later. Never even acknowledging the good luck such as having a crazy overgrown moose kid. Too busy always trying to cover your own behind.

*

While Sam dresses I run up the hill and climb the wooden back steps at the store, which, being covered with snow is like scaling a peak in Alaska. Each step is heaped with snow up to the next one. I go over to Artie's window and knock and wave. He lets out a big scream which brings Miss Ida running. She opens the back porch door, rifle at the ready.

"Marshall? That you? You're lucky to be alive. Come away from that window and get in here," she hollers. "Hold it: brush off real good first."

I am covered from head to toe with snow. Artie must've thought he'd seen the Abominable Snowman.

"For what are you out here at this hour? Somebody sick or something?" Miss Ida turns on a kettle of water. She has let me into her kitchen.

"It's Sam," I say. I'm still panting from the climb. "He's gotta plow. He needs help."

"I don't do no plowing," she says. I nod toward Artie who is standing there in his baby blue pajamas, rubbing his eyes.

"It's awful cold," she starts to protest. Then she orders Artie to get dressed. She says it will be good for him. As we leave she wraps him up tight in a hand knit muffler, a purple one which just happens to match his new maroon parka.

"Be careful," she warns him. Like we were off to the North Pole or something. She kisses him on the forehead and lets us out through the store. There's no need to risk Mount Everest twice.

By now only tiny snowflakes blow like dust in the air. The wind is down. Now and then the moon breaks out to shine on the chalky snow. There is dead silence, save a few tied-up half-frozen dogs that stir as we crunch and splash down the hollow and across the tracks towards Todd's house.

You can almost see the invisible line between us and them—the houses become smaller and older, tar paper replaces shingles on many shacks. I can count on one hand the times I have been here, though I can see down here from the window in my bedroom. It's a good thing Todd seems to know when to show up. I only went to his house one time. We were in sixth grade. We had a special project to work on for social studies—we had to make a relief map of the world.

I came down here and a woman opened the door—a heavy set woman with dirty brown hair.

"You want something?" she said.

"Todd here?"

The woman didn't say anything. She just closed the door in my face. Todd opened it a minute later.

"Come in, Marshall."

I had never been in a white person's house before. I don't know what I expected. I was surprised that it was so . . . plain. Bare yellow walls. A few sticks of furniture.

The woman who came to the door sat over at a sewing machine in the corner. She pumped the pedal like she was driving. The machine whirred and roared. Her fingers were laced up in there like it was them she was sewing.

"That's my mother," Todd said. "Mom, this is Marshall."

She nodded at me.

Back in Todd's room was a different story. He had plastered the walls with baseball posters and baseball cards and baseball stats. He was into the game back then. Before he found out it cost money he didn't have to join a team, and talent he didn't have to play.

We sat on his bed and plotted out the map on a big piece of cardboard he had. We would put the clay on later. Rose bought that for us. It was up at my house. After we'd worked for a while, Todd's mother brought us two glasses of milk and some cookies. I remember those Oreos were kind of stale.

Just before we finished I noticed that there was a man standing in the door. A tall man with red-blond hair. He didn't say a word. After he'd gone I heard Todd's mother call his name.

When he returned it was time for me to go. Todd walked me out the door and up the hill halfway to my house. He stopped me in the street a little past his house.

"That last window back there, see it?" He indicated it with his finger. "You ever need me, go straight there and tap. No one will bother you."

I was never invited back and he never said anything more about that day. Not much about the people behind the door either. Until recently. He acts like they don't exist. Like they are some kind of dirty secret.

Tonight we give Todd's system its first try. Both Artie and me hang back: everyone knows these folks down here keep hunting guns and pit bulls. I finally get the courage to go to the window, crouching low in the dark to do it. Artie hides behind a scraggly black walnut tree.

I tap on the window three times, cross my fingers, say a little prayer.

Todd squints out into the night. In the glass I can see him mouth my name as if it were a question. I beckon him with my hand. He points in a direction behind me and makes the word "depot" nice and clear. I nod and take off.

Artie and I hustle up the road and wait by an old abandoned railroad station. Sam says his granddaddy and them built this depot eighty years ago hoping to make the trains for the city stop. The train never stopped here. The tracks are pulled up now, and the only thing left is a beat-up booth covered with graffiti and a faded sign saying Washington Park.

Artie and I stand moving against the cold. Before I can find the place I've painted my own name, we hear, "What's up boys?"

I explain the situation and we start walking up Dorset Road. I suggest we go straight to the landfill. Sam'll already be there. I hope. As we cross King Drive I can make out Sam up ahead, on foot, heading for the shed.

I want to yell, "Hey, old man," but instead we just trot up the hill and fall in step at his side.

"Ready," I say.

Sam looks over his help. "Let's get to it," he nods.

I guess we'll do.

Inside the shed—which is just a large corrugated iron box really—the winter supplies are stuck in back behind lawn mowers and rakes. This storm, most unexpected, it seems, caught Sam unprepared. Around the walls, around the room, Sam's usually neat organization is showing the wear of the last few months. Crude white outlines on the pegboard wall suggest pitchforks or mallets, but there are no pitchforks or mallets to be seen. The dump truck is usually ready to go. I hope it is tonight.

Not quite: the snow blade needs to be hitched up. Sam takes over.

"First, get a shovel down for each of you. Couple of you clear that sidewalk out front and then run across the way and get the county office walk."

Todd grabs Artie saying "let's go," and they take off to do those jobs.

"Marshall, dig in the desk and find my map copies."

I go into the little office which is tacked onto the side of the shed like a lean-to. The desk top is inch-deep in paper—another victim of the times. I shuffle through the tangled invoices, the receipts for gasoline and repairs. In the middle drawer I find a stack of crude maps copied on white paper.

"Bring that here," he says. He lays the map on the running board. "Look at what I do here. I mark off the streets we clear, and the two sidewalks—get me a pen," he orders.

I do, and he marks an "X" through the walkways drawn in front of two squares on the copy.

"Assuming them boys get it done," he says.

"They will," I assure him.

"Good," he says. "What I do is I sign this form and run it over to the commisioner's office so they know I done my job. All folks care is the streets are clean and the garbage gets picked up. Best to have your proof, though."

Sam and I unload a bunch of fertilizer bags and rakes from the truckbed. Pretty quick Artie and Todd come in huffing and puffing.

"Done," Artie pants. He leans on a post clutching one side as if he were having some sort of spasm.

"Now we gotta get that blade over here." Sam says. He's got this down to some kind of a system. What system, I don't know.

It takes three of us on one side with Sam on the other, but we manage to haul it around to the front of the truck.

"On the count of three, lift her up and set her in these grooves here. I'll bolt her down."

Sam counts and we hoist our end, but the first time we miss the two slotted arms and drop the blade with a loud slam. It just misses Todd's foot.

"Son of a bitch," Todd says.

"Easy, boys," Sam laughs. "Take your time. Get a good grip. We'll try her again."

Sam counts again. The next time we are successful.

"That's the way she goes," he cheers. "While I tighten this up, you fellas clear the way to the back door — get all that mess out of the way. Then open the door and start shoveling those cinders into the bed."

So we do that. Todd and Artie team up to move giant bags of cement. Artie collapses on the pile of bags after the third or fourth one, but before I can go tell him how worthless he is, Todd signals me to help him finish moving them. Pretty soon Artie is up again carrying all the little stuff around — two empty buckets, a rake, a gallon of paint.

The rockpile out back looks like a giant scoop of ice cream. In order to get to the cinder and salt mixture we pull the plastic cover from the top. It is weighted with a layer of heavy, wet snow.

At first we go shovel by shovel, until Todd spies an old wheelbarrow. We fill it and then run it up to the truck bed on an old piece of board. Todd and I load, Artie runs and dumps.

A harsh roar cuts the silence as Sam fires up the big truck. He jumps out, tosses our makeshift ramp aside and backs the truck directly to the mound.

"Now we're in business," he announces. He grabs a shovel and starts heaping mounds of cinders into the truckbed. It looks as if to him they were as light as feathers.

"Fill her up," he adds. "It's from last year's budget and there's plenty." All three of our shovel loads wouldn't fill one of his. Simultaneously, almost as if we'd planned it, we three boys stop and lean on the shovels, taking a breath.

Sam lets out a belly laugh. "You not giving out on me yet?" he says. We dig back in.

The storm is completely over and the sky has taken on the purple blue of early morning. Our steamy breath rises into the sharp, clear air. Us boys sweat streams of water and have stripped down to sweaters and hats only. No one says anything, except Sam, who steams on unwinded, encouraging us with "just a little more" and "heap it up" and, finally, "last load."

Our job, then, is to ride in back, feeding cinders out of the truckbed, while Sam plows the lane. Sam creeps along slowly. The blade makes a loud scraping sound. Just as we start to relax, Sam orders us off the truck to clear an intersection, open up a curb, expose a fire hydrant.

"Can't you move that shovel no faster," he bullies. We are past caring with exhaustion.

*

Just as the sun pops up red, setting the fresh snow on fire, the truck jerks to a halt in front of Miss Ida's store. The cleared streets of Washington Park — Sam Finney's pride and joy — turn a defiant, cindery black eye to the new morning.

Inside the store it is already steamy warm, so thickly welcome warm almost to reach beneath the clothes and massage our tired muscles. Sam blusters in, wanting to know "what they've got in this joint for a hardworking man."

Betty Lou, behind the counter, points up the back steps to indicate there waits paradise. She and Sam exchange shy smiles, and though Todd and I wave at her, Artie rustles right on by without as much as a grunt. Betty Lou's eyes shut for just a quick moment, and I think I can even hear her heart break a little more. She bravely ushers us up the steps to the apartment.

On the table Miss Ida has set out cups of juice and hot chocolate. It seems as fast as we sit down, she sets a stack of pancakes at each place.

Sam quickly sips some coffee and says he'll eat later. He waves as he is leaving.

"I'll look after them," Miss Ida says down the steps.

The food knocks us out. No one remembers where we fell asleep, though sleep we do, soundly, not at all aware of the strong sun already melting all the snow from the steep roof just above our heads.

10

I'D NEVER SEEN Sam with a dustrag.

So on that day during winter break when I came out from my room because there was a commotion, my jaw about drops off.

"What are you doing?" I ask in a way that is more challenging than inquisitive.

"Cleaning up this joint," he says.

I ask him why. He says something about the joint needing it. Then he says real casual, "We may be having some holiday visitors."

It seems to me there are people in and out of this joint on a regular basis.

"I'm gonna be entertaining," he adds.

Now, Sam usually does most of his "entertaining" at various sundry locations such as Miss Ida's and—most importantly—at the Elks.

You know the Elks, down on the corner of Dorset and King, the big cinder-block box. It, together with Park Baptist, makes up what might be called downtown Washington Park.

In addition to a full selection of (so I'm told) watered-down drinks, an antique pinball machine, and a juke box featuring a lot of old-timey R & B records, the Elks is mainly a large parking lot in which a couple of dozen Caddies and pickups can park comfortably.

On Saturday night and a lot of other nights and days, too, every old geezer from Washington Park hangs out down there. The younger ones stay inside and play pool while the older folks stand outside near the mostly newer Cadillac Sevilles and run down the younger men inside.

Sam is at a rather transitional stage where sometimes you find him inside and sometimes out.

Sam says the Elks is a club, but as far as I can tell the only requirements to get in are a beer gut and good cash money.

I'm remembering the time when I was seven or so and Rose was looking for Big Sam for supper. She told me to run down to the Elks and tell him to do something such as get his butt home fast. Rose'd've gone herself except women aren't encouraged at the Elks. Ladies, that is. Women you can find: a certain Betty Lou Warner is known to be a frequent and a welcome guest.

So off little Marshall goes to fetch Big Sam.

Back in those days Sam was more of an inside man. I remember pulling open the heavy wooden door. In that door was a diamond-shaped yellow window, and the only bright light in the Elks entered through it. Once inside I felt like I'd entered a cave — everything was rich browns and reds, including all the clothes and skin. Red neon from Busch and Budweiser signs cast a hot glow on everything, and a bare yellow bulb swayed low over a pool table off to the side. Soupy stale air thick with smoke and smelling of beer filled my lungs. My eyes slowly adjusted to the dark as I looked around to find Big Sam.

Being just suppertime there weren't too many folks in there, except a half-dozen or so, clustered at the bar. A couple of these dudes were Sam's running buddies, and there was also this woman next to Sam. She wore a pink outfit. I recognized Sam as the tallest one and also as the focus of activity: he was showing-off — telling a story about some gangsters or something that had "junked an old car full of loot up at the dump." This tall tale had grown even since the last time I'd heard it, so I stood back and listened.

Sam goes on, "I got my feet up having some coffee and here comes this old dago in a fancy suit. 'Say boy' he says to me, and I says 'yassuh' and he asks if a couple of days ago did a couple of guys leave an old black Ford here and I look at him just like this here." Sam makes for all to see a dumb face with his lip let out low.

The pink woman laughed a loud horsey laugh. "You a crazy fool," she said. She slapped him on his upper arm. All the old boys laugh, too.

"Let me finish," Sam goes on. " 'Yassuh,' I says 'I seems to recollect a car just such as the one you speaking of,' and I shuffle off with him down back, you remember where I had all them old cars. A big rat come ("No, no," hollers the pink lady, grabbing Sam all up in his arm) a big rat about the size of a raccoon run out in front of us. That old dago boy took off – flew out of there." Sam bent over, moving his arms back and forth as if he was running.

"Just like that, he run. Come back the next day with two big heavy dudes. Guess he figured they'd save him from some damn rat."

The round of laughter was interrupted by one of Sam's cronies – an almond-colored man with hair only around the side of his head.

"Looky here," he said, nudging Sam and pointing to me. "They startin em younger every day."

I ran over quick and wrapped myself around one of Sam's legs. His hair was all black back then, and he wore his favorite outfit from those days: jeans, a jean jacket and an old yellow-brimmed "CAT" hat. He didn't take to overalls until he got that belly.

"Here's Mister Marshall," he said. He hoisted me up to sit on the bar. "I thought we'd cut you off from drinking." He put me right where the pink lady stood. She'd moved down to the end of the bar.

I told him, "Mama says you gotta come home right now for supper." That caused a lot of snickering in the crowd.

"Does she now?" Sam laughed. "Well, you and I ain't quite finished our beer." He lifted the glass to my lips and I sipped the warm liquid. It was bitter and I made a face. "That's right," he said. "Nasty."

There was a lot of talk around the bar such as "put some hair on his chest" and "chip off the old block."

When I was that age Sam seemed bigger and more powerful than anyone in the world. He slung me off that bar and right up to his shoulders as we took his leave. I had to duck down as we cleared the door with the gold diamond window. I bet between us we were eight feet tall.

*

Big Sam's guest arrives just before supper. Sam has fixed a platter of breaded chops, made gravy of the drippings and mashed a bowl of potatoes. He's opened a can of peas and I've even been asked to make a little salad. "Add a nice touch," he says, but we almost never eat salad. Ever. Sam's all fired-up, so I do as I'm told.

Sam's all dolled up, too: he's wearing his beige dress pants with the new striped red and white shirt I got him for Christmas. (X-large, 18½,

35). When the doorbell rings Sam quick throws on his navy blazer, straightens his cuffs and opens the door.

"Come right on in. Let me rest your coat."

She is wearing a waist-length blue fur which was made from something with impossibly long hair. I mean, this coat — you could braid the hair on this mother. She has a matching silk scarf tied under her chin to protect her hair. She pulls off the coat and pulls the scarf back through one of the sleeves.

Sam hands the pile to me. It is like holding an armload of feathers. It smells like flowers.

"Miss Annie B. Semple, this is my son, Marshall. I told you all about him."

"Evening, Miss Semple," I say.

"Please to meet you, sugar. Call me Annie B. Everybody does." She says this in a voice that is high and sweet.

"Take her things in the other room there," Sam says to me, and then to her, "Make yourself to home. Have a seat."

While I'm hanging her coat, she accepts Sam's offer of "a cool one." I lean on the door jamb and give her the double O. She's eased back on the plaid sofa real casual with her legs crossed, but the thing is — they're only sort of crossed as if there were some sort of problem with them. As if the one leg couldn't quite figure out how to get across the other one. She's got on a green dress, and next to her medium brown skin it makes her look like she's sickly. Annie B. hasn't stopped smiling since she walked in — grinning really — raising up these big brown cheeks and forcing dimples into them.

The whole effect — the round head circled with curls, the little green slippers — the whole effect is somehow soft and jolly. She is like a clown at the circus.

Before I can volunteer, Sam says, "Entertain our guest while I set out dinner." Sam goes and gets his table ready. He is determined this be a one man show.

"I hear you in high school."

"Yes, ma'am — a junior."

"No need to ma'am me, sugar. Come over and sit by me." I do. She raises a fleshy arm up behind me and pulls me over. "This sure is a cute place you all have."

This is a crackerbox. It has a broken glass table and a large broken

99

mirror, though the mirror, the way Sam cracked that, looks like it could have been meant to be that way. Sam has fanned out the sections of today's *Post Dispatch* so as to cover the main line of the crack on the table.

I don't say any of this. Instead I say:

"Thank you," and then ask her where she lives, the polite conversational thing to do.

"Up in Overland. You know that area?"

I tell her I do. It's one of those places with poor people and crackerbox houses just like here in Washington Park. Except the poor people up there think their shit don't stink.

A crackerbox is a crackerbox.

We sit there in silence a long, long time — I simply cannot think of a thing to say to her. She is contentedly sucking at the beer can like a baby with a fresh nipple.

Sam saves us at last. "Come and get it."

I sit down at the table and put on my best eating manners: elbows up, free hand in the lap with the napkin. One never really enjoys food with guests because of all these rules.

Imagine my surprise: Sam and Annie B. stuff napkins in their collars and dig in — start greasing. They pick up pork chop bones to tear the meat off. They suck and slurp until the bones are bare. They shovel mounds of gravied mashed potatos into their mouths and heap up seconds and thirds while I'm still on my first pork chop.

The thing is, I'm mesmerized. By the sound, even. The grunting, moaning and general "mmm, mmm, mmm-ing."

"Something wrong with your food?" Sam wants to know of me.

"It's just great," I say, though it's really only just fair. A lot of salt, a lot of flour, a lot of grease. I quick eat what's on my plate. It's the last of the meat. I eat it before one of them asks me for it.

For twenty minutes that's all the talk there is except for an occasional "pass me the peas" or "sure is good." And in just that much time they are done, leaned over to the side in their chairs, puffing and panting. Eventually they are able to haul themselves out and sit in front of the TV.

The tabletop looks like dogs have eaten here. Little chunks of potato, explosions of gravy, trails of green peas. I am stunned. I clean it away before anyone can see.

"Sure is nice of him to clean that kitchen," Annie B. shouts, intending that I hear.

"He's a good boy," Sam shouts in response.

They watch Cosby and whisper and giggle the evening away.

*

I wake up shocked in the middle of the night. What could there be left to eat? How could they be at it again?

Opening the door to my room I discover the house dark and realize I am wrong. What sounds like eating is another matter entirely.

Can you imagine? That's what it sounds like here. Sloppy and gross. When you go to the movies and the good part comes on, there is all this music playing. Who's ever listening to it, anyway. But who could imagine this? It could be a zoo in there, or people unloading crates at the warehouse. The squeak of the bedsprings. The giggles.

I heard Rose giggle once.

Oh, my God.

I lay back down, close my eyes and try to sleep. It's hot in the room so I open a window, and then it's cold and I shiver. I'm sick to my stomach but I really haven't eaten anything. I pray for relief of any kind. Nothing happens, and years later morning brightens my room.

*

After the first visit Sam stops me in the kitchen.

"What do you think of my lady?"

Before I can answer he nudges me in a disgusting way saying, "Ain't she something else?" He laughs heartily.

"She sure is something," I say flatly.

Sam goes on to tell me how Annie B. is the sort of person who just makes you feel good, a person who is always happy, a person you don't have to say nothing entertaining to or nothing.

I nod.

Sam says he's lucky—damn lucky—to find one of the good ones.

"Lotsa dogs out there," he says. "Man can't be too careful nowadays."

I nod some more.

"You don't mind my lady spending the night," Sam asks me. Straight out he asks me.

"No, sir," I say. He pats me on the back and says "Good man," or

IOI

some such thing. As if I were, in some way, more a part of this little deal than an innocent bystander. And what if I'd said "yes," anyway.

And slowly Annie B. Semple works her way under my skin. The voice becomes syrupier and grating. Her brown skin shines, seems to soak up all the light in the room. And she sits there with that stupid smile, waiting for me to serve her "a cold one" or some Doritos. One night she watches me boil a can of soup for my dinner. She and Sam are headed off to some fancy place for steak and shrimp. Sam says she likes romantic joints. Annie B. sticks a finger in my soup.

"Needs salt, sugar," she says.

*

About this time I get another letter from Rose. She encloses it in a Christmas card. The Santa on the card wears shorts and sunglasses.

Dear Marshall:

Things go like they go. I get by. Which I guess is what this is all about.

Everything's upside down. It's freaky. Eggs . . . make eggs for just yourself for the first time and it's like you've never eaten eggs before. You go to the store and get whatever you want. Whatever you got the money for. Don't worry about what Sam has a taste for. Or what Marshall won't eat. I get sad about that, too.

I got me a job. A little old piece a one, Sam'd call it. Waitressing in a coffee shop at the Sahara Hotel. Believe that. I got me a silly little uniform. A short little skirt and a little cap says "Debbie" on it. Debbie musta had the job before me. A lot of those dudes you don't want to know your real name no how.

Christmas was a bitch. I worked. These places never close. Pouring out coffee to folks that looked as lost as I felt.

Me and some of the other girls got together and grilled steaks and exchanged gifts.

Barbecue on Christmas!

Terri, who wants to be a dancer, got drunk and cried. I cried, too.

Everybody here wants to be something else. Unless they're already Wayne Newton or Cher. Everybody wants to meet a rich man, sing, get famous. We wished each other all our dreams to come true.

I cried cause I didn't even know what my dreams were yet.

At least I'm some place warm. And I got a nice silk scarf and a bottle of Shalimar.

Nevada is not like Missouri at all. It is hot, dry, flat, sandy. Out in the distance there are mountains, yet try driving out to them and they seem to move away. It's almost like they aren't there at all. Christmas in the desert does not seem like Christmas at all. I pretend by watching the holiday specials. I recreate the Christmases of my memory.

When you were just a little thing Sam and me would hide your gifts and then sneak them out late at night. We thought you'd believe in Santa forever. Such a cute thing, opening up gifts in your pajamas. One year Sam didn't get paid till Christmas Eve. We drove all over the county looking for an open store. We got you a flat wooden train and you loved it.

Remember?

Check this out: I was in the hotel lobby and across the way I saw a boy from the back. This boy has the same hair as you and even a sweatshirt like the kind you like to wear. I ran and hid behind a giant plastic palm plant. Then he was gone.

I know it wasn't you but for a minute I thought you'd come for me. Would you do that?

And don't ask me what I was hiding from. Hiding maybe cause this is my thing out here. I don't know how you fit into it yet.

I'll let you know when I got it down.

> *Later,*
> *Mother.*

Annie B. spies me rereading my letter. "What's that?"

"A letter," I say. "From my mother." I try to say it nice. Whatever way I say it, for once her big smile almost completely disappears. What was left was as false as a warm winter day.

*

One night the Finney bladder fills on schedule, so I go to deal with it and am waylaid by a light from the kitchen.

"Hee hee," giggles Annie B.. "You caught me." She has spread before her a regular smorgasbord of delights: paper-thin slices of ham, hunks of Velveeta, a salami, sweet pickles.

"Just making myself a little bedtime treat."

For the Chicago Bears. Of course I don't say that. She's sitting there, her hair all rolled up and pinned into little knots. She's thrown on a nightgown that is pink and covered with little hearts.

"Join me?"

I shake my head, which she thinks means "no," but really means "give me a break." I swear: between her and Sam they've put on 55 pounds. You'd think all they did was eat.

Unfortunately I know that's not true.

I don't see any other choice but to discuss this matter with my boys.

"What I know of your dad," Todd offers, "he wouldn't be really thrilled about you dipping into his business."

"She's eating us out of house and home."

"Bullshit," Todd says.

"All I know is a man has certain needs," Artie begins, but since fists are against the newly established rules, Todd and I ignore him.

As if someone like him knew what a man needed.

I go on as if he hadn't spoken, "It's all true. All of it."

I tell them about the last straw. That was when I found Annie B. in the kitchen at 3:45 in the morning in some sort of hypnotic trance. She'd forgotten her robe. She was wearing only a green silky see-through thing. I mean, I could see everything. There were layers and layers of it. Somehow it never looks the way you remember it. The way it looks in those magazines. It is always a shock, isn't it? Artie and Todd and I found one of them magazines once. Up by the depot. This didn't look like that at all. There was a lot more of this, and this was a lot more . . . loose.

So there all of Annie B. was, stirring rhythmically a bowl of fudge cake mix. The box was torn open and the floor was covered with egg shells. The water splashed in the sink for background noise. It was like the Night of the Living Dead. I went in there and shook her. "Miss Annie, Miss Annie," I said. She came-to with a start and then was all embarassed.

I asked her what she was doing, but she ran back to the bathroom, trying to cover herself, using these chocolate stained hands.

I tell them I'd made up my mind then and there that sleep-eating was not to be tolerated in Washington Park.

The boys agree that this is completely unacceptable and surely dangerous; that any night Sam and I might be flambéd in our sleep. But what to do.

"I'm telling you," says Todd, "your old man probably couldn't care if she stood on her head naked as a jaybird on the front lawn and whistled Dixie." His country-boy way of saying: this must be love.

And I pray right then and there it is something else, something, whatever other choices there are.

We decide that I have to set her up; that the best idea is to let old Sam see her for what she really is. All Sam needs is to see the cow standing in his kitchen, half-asleep, making Malt-O-Meal pancakes. That'll fix her.

But Annie B. does not show up for a few days. And the next couple of times she does, she sleeps through the night. Or I do.

One afternoon Sam comes in and finds me cooking my dinner. He seems tense. "Annie ain't been here, has she?"

He seems relieved when I say "no."

"Do me a favor," he says. "She calls, say I'm out."

"There a problem?" I ask him.

"You know how these things go."

I don't, but I play along.

Annie B. is around a few more times before it runs its course; I didn't have to do a thing. That last night Sam sat there on the couch and said nothing to her. Nothing.

Maybe he got tired of feeding her or maybe she got tired of his silence. Whatever — she just disappeared. Sam never said a word about her again.

*

The advantage of the front of the parade is you are in a better position to be remembered.

After Annie B. there is Judy, the nurse from Barnes Hospital. And a truck driver for U.P.S. whose name I can't remember, just as I can't remember the name of the woman with the twin girls. The little girls' names are Deidre and Desiree, and the U.P.S. woman, due to her uniform, was all the same color — dark brown.

There is a taxi dispatcher. She shows me a gun she keeps tucked in her purse.

Tall and wide women. Skinny and yet still wide women. Thin hair, stringy hair, and every color black comes in women: café au lait, ebony, light brownskin, dark brownskin, all the yellows, pinks and beiges, too. Sam keeps em three hours, three days, three weeks: what was Sam looking for, anyway?

At the kitchen table late one night, Sam in the door, me in a trigonometry book:

"Marshall, do you ever get lonely?"

I don't look at him. I don't answer him. I don't say a word.

There's this thing about Sam's eyes: they look one way for people he goes for, and a different way when he don't give a damn. Those eyes practically change colors, to tell you the truth — wax museum glass eyes changed to real ones and back again. Hot eyes and cold eyes.

Only a few times did Sam's eyes cool. Really, I think almost all of them could have stayed forever. A whole house full of mothers.

As if he loved each and every one.

II

"I'd like this class to do something special for parents' night." Miss O'Hare says. "I want us to do a reading and a panel discussion of our essays."

Doesn't that sound like fun.

For spring semester Todd and I have signed up for a class that Miss O'Hare is offering only for juniors: Telling Your Heart's Truth. Ohairy says the purpose of this class is for us to explore our values and ideas, and to learn how to express them with enthusiasm and clarity.

It's a composition class.

"Your assignment is to pick one of our 'burning issues' (a list of gripes, disasters, tragedies, and complaints posted in front of the room) and fully explore it in a three to five page paper."

Acid rain. World hunger. Deforestation. There isn't too much up on that list I get excited about. Where are all the good topics? Such as: Why is my teacher getting on my nerves? and, What is it that makes parents so obnoxious?

"I want your parents to hear what's on your minds."

There are usually about twelve of us here for this class. I don't know most of them, but Todd does. These are the new Kathleen O'Hare groupies. All the smart and quiet kids. The popular crowd—Connie Jo, Buzz, and all them—took Mr. McLaughlin's class. You can get an A in there if you spell your name right on your paper. They spend their time hanging out in the library, planning the school dances, going about their business like usual. Here I sit with a bunch of funeral directors. These people are *so* serious. There's hardly any laughter.

"Parents' night is March twelfth. Remind your folks, I want a big turnout."

At long last the bell rings.

"See you guys tomorrow. We'll be talking about Amnesty International. Don't forget your report, Todd."

Did I see what I saw? When we walked by her desk?

"I won't."

Did she just pat him on the ass?

*

"Boring," I scream. We are standing out by Artie's car waiting for him to show up. He and Susan have to do a couple of laps around the hall at the end of the day. All the couples do that. To show off.

No, she would never do anything like that. It's my imagination acting weird again.

"Your mind has just turned to crap, Marshall. All that television you watch."

"Well. At least that's entertaining. Why does everything have to be so . . . heavy." I drop my head when I say 'heavy.' See if I can get some reaction out of him.

"You're incapable of taking anything seriously, aren't you."

"Here comes old Artie." Old Artie strolls out the front door like he owns the joint.

"Everything's got to be a joke for you. You already know everything in the whole damn world."

If I clench my fist real tight, I will not pop him in the mouth.

"Afternoon, fellas," Artie says. He is grinning ear to ear. "Sorry to keep you waiting."

"What, you get lost on the way to the car again?" I ask.

"Marshall is in one of his moods," Todd says.

"We got to get him a woman," Artie says. He and Todd laugh gross hyena laughs.

"You know, I'll stop this car and kick both your asses."

They both just laugh some more, so I lean back in the back seat and put my feet up so that my left foot is by Artie's head and the right foot is by Todd.

"P. U." That from Artie. "Don't you ever change your socks? I get fresh socks put out every morning."

"Marshall is protecting the environment. He's saving wash water."

They laugh some more. I stick my feet closer, right up in their faces.

*

After Artie drops us off, Todd walks down the hill with me.

"So, what are we gonna write about?"

"We?"

"I told Kathy you and me would work together. I guess I forgot to mention that."

"I don't even know if I'm doing this stupid assignment."

"Sure you are. And you're just saying it's stupid because you're too lazy to put any effort into thinking about it."

"I got a lot on my mind. Down here at the house and all." I nod up toward where I live.

Todd comes all up in my face. "You got it pretty hard, huh." He says this as if I were a puppy or a little boy. He even pats me on the arm. "I'll be up after supper. You think of something to write on. Before I get there."

*

As I go to turn the key in the lock, it's as if it has a life of its own. The knob turns, and I'm actually pulled by the door into the crackerbox.

"Hi there. I mean, I heard your key in the door so I thought I'd . . . I mean, Sam told me to expect you . . ."

She says all this as I'm trying to wiggle my key out of the lock. She's got a shaggy wet lettuce balled up in a long, blue striped apron. I follow her back to the kitchen where she drops the lettuce into a beige plastic bowl.

"Towels? Paper towels?" She shrugs and waves her hands around. "Where do you keep them?"

I reach under the sink and hand her a fresh package.

"Great. Thanks." She rips off the plastic then tears off a hunk of towels. She starts rolling the ball of lettuce around the bowl.

"Pig grass, they call this in Europe. You couldn't give it away." She balls up the towels and hoops them over toward the trash can. Just as quick she grabs my hand and squeezes it between the two of hers.

"Gayle," she says.

*

So this time it's Gayle.

I have to give her credit: usually they take their time, worm their way in. This gal's walked right in, made herself at home.

What do you do when there's someone you don't know in your kitchen and they're . . . doing stuff? This sort of thing's been the rule around here of late — always folks you don't really know in the bathroom, in the kitchen, elsewhere. And since they're not your guests, there's not a whole lot you can say to them. Yet, you have all these questions. Like: why are you here? And what do you think you're doing?

"Can I help you with something?" I ask.

"Can you make lemonade?" she asks. "It'd be just the thing with dinner." She hands me lemons from a grocery bag on the table. As she hands me the lemons she looks me right in the eyes, all around in my face — gives me the double O.

"Use what you need," she says, and I drop two or three of them to the floor.

"Sorry," I say. She giggles at my clumsiness.

I sit at the dinette table, cut the lemons in half and begin squeezing them into a pitcher. Gayle, at the sink, uses her hands to rip the lettuce to shreds. "May I?" she asks. She takes one of the lemons and squeezes some of the juice onto the cut up lettuce.

"I'll finish the salad nearer to suppertime."

"We don't eat much salad," I tell her.

"That's true of too many black folks," she says. "It would be a good idea to add a lot of raw fresh food to your diet. Think about it."

I nod politely, think to myself, damn — one of those know-it-all types. One who still hasn't told me what she's doing here in my kitchen fixing dinner. Whatever's on the stove sure smells good, though.

"May I ask what we're having for supper?"

"Yes, you may ask," she says. She makes my "may" sound childish. "I'm cooking Groundnut Stew, an African dish made with peanut butter."

"Ick."

"Come on and give it a try," she says, laughing. "There's plenty of salad if it's that nasty. Come here," she orders. She takes the lid off the pot, spoons up a little and aims it at my mouth.

I run the brown liquid over my tongue quickly and swallow. It leaves behind the taste of pepper, cinnamon, some things I don't recognize. And peanuts, too.

"Be honest," Gayle prompts.

I shrug and nod my head.

Gayle shoves me on the shoulder. "What's that supposed to mean? This some of that good down home cookin — probably prevents cancer, too. Say something about it."

"It's different. Sam and I are sort of meat and potato types."

"I bet that Sam eats anything put in front of him," she says. "And there's plenty of salad for him, too."

As if on cue, himself comes in the front door.

"Speak of the devil," Gayle says, raising her eyebrows at me.

Sam comes back to the kitchen. He says a quiet "Hi" to each of us. He's acting all shy and stuff.

"I see you've met," he says.

Gayle gives Sam a little peck on the cheek on the way to the fridge. She rubs at the half-moon indentation on the door. Then she points at me and says to Sam. "That's something else you've got there."

"Don't I know it," Sam says. He goes over to the stove and opens the stew pot. Behind Gayle's back he gives me a frightened look, as if his eyes will pop out of his head.

*

Sam and Gayle disappear after the dishes are done. Todd shows up a little while later, notebook in hand.

"So, partner, what's it gonna be?"

"How about: What I did on my summer vacation."

"Get serious."

"I am serious. I have a real exciting life. I go to the mall at least once a week. My mom's crazy, she ran off and lives in the desert. My dad has a new girlfriend every week. People enjoy reading this sort of thing."

"I mean it, Marshall. You are going to have to get real. If you and I are gonna stay friends." He looks at me over his glasses like he was my grandpa or something. Real serious and stern.

"Okay," I say.

I wonder if it's worth it.

"Because we're working together we have to do five or six pages for the grade. I got some ideas, if you want to hear them."

"Five or six? What happened to three?"

"Look, I don't need this grade at all. I've already done enough extra credit."

Extra credit. Snicker, snicker, snicker.

"Whatever," I say.

Todd takes over. "I thought I'd like to focus on nuclear waste this time. How does that sound?"

"Great," I say.

I know as much about nuclear waste as I do about nuclear physics.

"Kathy and I were thinking this might be just the issue to bring the community together."

"Why should anybody around here care about it?"

"Duh, Marshall. They ship that stuff all over the place. On trains. In trucks. What if there was a derailment? What if some of it spilled? No, better. What if it got left in the dump? What would you do then?"

I shrug. The dump is Sam's problem.

"If you knew more, you'd worry more. Let's get to it. Let's make a list of all the reasons why we're against it. You write."

I do.

This is how it goes for the entire project. Todd spouts off at the mouth and I write it down. I go "Oh, yeah, oh, yeah," every now and then, so he thinks I'm really into it. I, of course, get stuck with all the organizing into a final paper. Todd's no good at that. He gets too excited. His writing sounds hysterical.

I get stuck with the typing, too. I do it on Rose's electric that she kept in the back of the linen closet. It has a dark brown case, tortoise-shell hard.

The last thing we have to do is memorize all this so we can present it on parents' night. Why we're bothering, I'll never know, because Sam don't go to that stuff — that was Rose's job and Lord knows the P.W.T. haven't set foot in a school, probably not in their entire lives.

So, there I am getting dressed to go up to Eisenhower. Todd and I have hitched a ride from Artie and Miss Ida. Artie and his crowd are putting on a little play or the special olympics or something. It's better than taking the bus at least.

"Where you off to?" Sam wants to know.

"A thing at school," I say.

"What kind of thing?"

"Parents' night."

"Hang on there," he says. "Just one cotton-pickin minute."

He gets a goofy smile on his face and goes strutting back to his room. A few minutes later he comes strutting back out. He's changed into some slacks and a shirt. He looks sort of presentable.

"You're going to this?" I say. "You never go to this stuff."

"It's a new day," he says. He twirls his keys indicating it's time to go.

We pick up the others up at the store. They all pile into the truck with us. Miss Ida rides in the cab, and us boys sprawl out in the truckbed. It is a beautiful night, clear and warm. It's just after dark when we go. We lie on our backs and watch the new leaves on the trees flash by overhead.

At school there aren't many people at Miss O'Hare's event. Just a few of the parents of a few of the people from our composition class. And Sam. He sits right up front by the teacher's desk. That's where Todd and I sit to give our report.

Ohairy, who is standing by the doorway, leaning against the frame, nods for us to begin.

"Thank you for coming," Todd says. "Marshall and I are going to share some facts with you about nuclear waste."

I stammer, trying to remember my first line. I can remember something about the need for people to be informed, so I say something like that. I look at my notes a lot, which we aren't supposed to do. Todd says it is lot more effective to say it from memory, but if I look up I'm afraid Sam will be looking at me. I see him once or twice. He's got one finger on his chin. He looks concerned.

Finally, Todd says, "and, so in conclusion, the problem of nuclear waste is one that is easy to ignore, though doing so will not make it go away. Not for thousands and thousands of years. Thank you very much."

The few people in the room applaud. Todd beams.

"Any questions?" Miss O'Hare asks.

Mercifully, there are none.

"I want to thank you parents for coming," Ohairy says. "As a follow-up to tonight's discussion, my students will be looking into the problem of nuclear waste disposal. You may be hearing from us about some upcoming events. Feel free to visit and look around our school."

Sam is standing there waiting for us with a big grin going. He shakes my hand and Todd's hand.

"You boys done good," he says. "Seem to know what you're talking about."

I can't spend too much time basking in his praise because I can see Ohairy waiting for us at the door.

"Hello," she says, real enthusiastic. "You must be Marshall's dad. I can really see the resemblance."

"This is Miss O'Hare." I mumble it. "My father, Mr. Finney."

"It's a real pleasure," Sam says. He says it with this real smooth, deep voice. "A pleasure indeed. Call me Sam." He shakes her hand entirely too long.

"I'm with them, too," Todd says. Ohairy smiles at him.

"I'm so glad to meet you, Sam. Marshall has been in my classes for a couple of years now."

"How's the boy doing?"

I start dragging him toward the door. He balks.

"He's plenty bright, but I'm sure you know how he is. Getting Marshall to think sometimes is like pulling teeth."

"That's him, all right."

"We got some people to meet, right Todd." I'm hoping he'll get on the other side and help drag Sam out of there, but he is too busy sneaking grins.

I manage to get him moving toward the door.

"Let me know if he's one bit of trouble," Sam shouts.

"Nice meeting you," Ohairy says.

"My pleasure indeed. Indeed."

*

We round up Artie and Miss Ida and get Sam back to the truck. He is having a great evening. He drives us to Dairy Queen and springs for treats.

After we drop the others off, Sam coasts down the hill from the store.

"Good work tonight, son."

"Thanks."

"Sounds like you're doing pretty good out there. You keep it up. Watch your step."

"It's not as hard as it looks."

"That's your teacher, huh? That nice one? The one I met."

"She's one of them."

"I see," he says. "Nice looking little gal."

I put a hand up by the side of my face to hide from him the sick look that comes over me. This man never quits.

"Umph, umph, umph. Nice looking gal indeed."

*

This Gayle decides to teach Sam the right way to cook. She says a person doesn't need all that fat, all that canned crap. Says that a man ought to be able to take care of himself better than that.

Sounds good to me.

"Lord help me," Sam says, but he comically rolls his eyes when he says it, and joins her in the kitchen without hesitation.

Lord help us indeed.

This is a Sunday dinner they're cooking, a Sunday late in March. I stand in the pass-through bar and watch.

"Pay attention, you," Gayle orders me. "I'm gonna stuff up this chicken."

"Not a damn chicken again." Sam throws up his hands. "I swear to God this girl here don't cook nothing else. Am I right?" he says to me. He pretends to walk away, but she tells him to hush and orders him to pull all the skin off the meat. She gives us a lecture about how blacks eat too much red meat, too much salted meat. Tells us we got to be responsible for our own health.

Gayle's always saying this stuff—stuff you have to wonder how she knows it. Still, it sounds true to me. That could be the way she says it. She's playful, so that even someone such as me who hates nothing worse than a show-off—says to himself, "Well, maybe."

She's even got Big Sam in there wrapping sweet potatos in foil. He's carrying on like a fool, too. He tears off the tiniest piece of foil he can and then starts winding it around the potato as if he were wrapping a mummy.

"Like this?" he asks.

Gayle looks at him with one eye closed. She purses her lips and rewraps the potato in almost one perfect motion. "Like that," she says. She cuts her eyes back and forth from me to him with a fake-evil, squinch-eyed smile.

Sam looks at me, bright-eyed, suppressing his laugh. He bites his lips and points at her.

*

Gayle tells a story at dinner about how she traveled with a hospital unit when she was in the army.

"I was on a burn team. We would move from base to base, as needed. Following a crash or an explosion, working on special cases. On-call twenty-four hours a day."

"It sounds like hard work," I say.

"I enjoyed it. If we could get to a site soon enough, we could make a big difference in a patient's recovery. I saw a lot of this country. A lot of the world."

I ask her what she remembered most.

"All the different kinds of people out there. What I loved most was that wherever you went, if you saw a black face and caught an eye, there'd be a warm response. I felt at home all over the world."

Her talking starts Sam talking, too.

"I haven't been much beyond the Saint Louis area," he says. "Missed Vietnam. That enlisting place over in Clayton . . . you believe they didn't want no blacks in the sixties. Back in the early days of the war. Wadn't even good enough to shoot at back then. A lot of us went anyway. When they got desperate for bodies."

"You could do without a trip like that," Gayle says.

We are eating the chicken that she . . . that we all made. It is baked, and covered with spices.

"We went down to the Ozarks once, didn't we Marshall?"

I nod.

"Stayed about a half a minute." Sam laughs. He looks distracted. He doesn't tell her how Rose wouldn't stay because there was a spider in the cabin, and because it was too hot, and because she was bored.

Gayle watches Sam quietly. When she's not eating she rests her chin on her hands. She makes a bridge, her elbows on the edge of the table.

Her round brown head sits on those hands and looks from Sam to me, like she was looking for a connection.

Sam goes on with his tale:

"When I was coming up folks just didn't go off places. Everybody stayed right here, visited with neighbors. You know what I mean?"

"But I bet sometimes you wanted to go away," Gayle says. "Everyone wants to see the world."

"Not me," Sam says. "I know Washington Park ain't much, but I've always liked it here. You can get too far from home, you know. When I was little a big day was going in to the city — going shopping down to the big Famous and Stix stores. Nowadays I don't know," he says sadly.

Gayle reaches over and pats Sam's arm.

Sam puts one of his hands on top of hers.

12

A SHIPMENT OF spent nuclear fuel is scheduled to pass Eisenhower High School on April first. Todd and Miss O'Hare are shocked when they get an endorsement — albeit cool — from the administration for the protest they are planning. It seems not even the big shots in the central office are too crazy about having this stuff come so close to the school. Seems not even the suits believe the government safety assurances. Though Ohairy would rather not tailor the demonstration to the school's regulations — thirty minutes max, no profanity, no damage to property — she and Todd are pleased with the respectability that comes with official recognition. They expect a big turnout. They can save the real stuff for next time, she says.

Todd comes up with the idea of a die-in. He says what we'll do is have a bunch of people in the field out by the fence — dancing and playing and other stuff. When the train passes we'll all fall down dead and then rise as skeletons and zombies. Ohairy thinks this is a great idea, real "telegenic," just the sort of thing that shows up good on the six o'clock news.

Mr. Shannon adds one other catch: you have to have your parents' permission to be out of school.

*

"This is gonna be lots of fun," Artie says, driving home. "I know just what I'm gonna wear, too. Can you wear whatever you want?"

"Jesus," mumbles Todd. For some reason he's grumpy.

"You see what I mean," I say. "A demonstration is just like a big party for these folks. Do you think they even know why we're going out there? Hell, no. What's this for?" I challenge Artie. "Why are you going out to the fence?"

"There's dangerous stuff coming by school. Where it could hurt kids. We don't want that, right?"

"Dangerous stuff. Lions and tigers and bears," I laugh. But Todd pats Artie on the shoulder and tells him that he's right. He tells him he appreciates the support.

*

Walking down from the store Todd's real sullen, and I figure with my big mouth I've done it again. So I go to covering my behind.

"Okay, so maybe people don't need to know all the facts about things to get involved in them. There probably isn't time; people should act on their feelings." All the crap we get in Ohairy's class.

"Marshall, I need a big favor."

"Just ask."

"There's no way my parents are gonna sign any permission."

And he knows that I know what he's going to ask. And already he starts begging—as if I were going to say no, which I wouldn't.

At least I don't think I would.

"It'll be just this once, and there's no way we'll get caught." He says this with a catch in his voice; what sounds almost like shame.

"Just tell me what you want it to say."

He says "thanks" and, though he's relieved, I can tell he's still upset about forging the note.

We walk up to my place. Gayle is there again. I introduce Todd. She gives Todd a long, friendly handshake, looking him right in the eye.

"Pleased to meet you," she says.

Todd gets all red in the face and embarrassed. All he can manage to say is "Hi." Gayle has that effect on you. She can look at me and make me feel like I ain't got no clothes on. It's like, one look from her, and she knows everything about you.

I tell her we've got homework to do. She says it's my house, and goes back to kitchen duty.

Todd wants the permission written on a crinkled piece of notebook paper. I try to write left-handed, but can't, so I write with the paper at an angle. We decide that that changes my scrawl just enough. I put it down as follows:

Todd has our permission to go to the event.

I sign it Mrs. Walter Lawrence. Todd looks it over and pronounces it okay.

"I wish my folks were different," he says.

"Don't we all," I say. Maybe for only the third time in our lives here is Todd talking about the P.W.T.

"I hate that they're so ignorant."

"I don't know anybody whose . . ."

"Just shut up . . ." Todd holds a shaking hand between us. He puts the hand to his forehead as if to still it. Or himself. Then he gets his composure back. He asks me to hold the note till tomorrow. He's acting as if we'd just robbed the First National Bank.

*

After Todd leaves, I go in to be polite to Gayle. It's still hard to get used to someone else around a lot. Someone who is not just Sam.

"That a good friend of yours?" she asks.

I tell her a really good friend. About the best.

She nods, and I can tell that she doesn't think there's anything funny at all about that. A lot of folks would. That is, the fact that a black kid and a P.W.T. would be friends. She acts like it is the most normal thing in the world.

Today she is chopping up vegetables, but pretty quick she stops. She wipes her hands and comes out to the living room. She picks up a magazine to read—one she's brought with her, an *Essence* magazine. We never have magazines around here.

I stand there with my arms crossed.

"You don't have to entertain me, Marshall."

I fumble around in the kitchen to make it look like I'm supposed to be doing something.

"If you feel the need to be here," she comes over and guides me, "then sit down and let's talk."

"Sam would be mad if I didn't . . ."

She waves a hand at me. "People don't need an excuse to talk. If you want to, cool. If not, that's cool, too."

Even though I can see right through her, I kinda like the way she says this stuff — like she's got hurt feelings, only not really. All Sam's gals have a certain style. You either like it or you don't. I am starting to like hers. It won't kill me to sit there for a while.

"Tell you what," she says. "Ask me something about myself. We'll take turns."

I decide to start with a hard one. "Where did you meet Sam?" I've been dying to ask that. Really, I want to ask all of Sam's gals that. Who knows where he finds them. There must be some trick to it.

Gayle looks at me as if she's wondering what kind of question that is.

"I had an old refrigerator in my way," she starts out. "It'd been my folks before mine. I'm telling you, it wasn't worth nothing. I didn't know what to do with it. Couldn't just leave the old dear out on the curve.

"I came by the dump and asked your dad if I could leave her there and he said 'yes.' Then I asked him if he'd come and get it for me. First he said 'hell, no.' Then he just came by and he got her out of there. The two of us did, actually. Sam just showed up. And afterwards, he asked me out."

She giggles like that was real funny. She asks me does that answer my question.

I ask her why'd she want to go out with a trash man, anyway.

She pats my arm, looks me right in the eye. She keeps looking at me with this smile on her face, a haughty smile that makes me shudder.

"I wanted to go out with *Sam,*" she says. For a while she says nothing else. She looks away almost as if she were embarrassed.

Finally she says, "Your turn. Time to tell me about you."

"Nothing to tell."

"Just plain old dumb boring Marshall?"

Which is not what I said. All these women — Sam's gals — they all want to know stuff about you. I figure it's their job. Just like, according to Sam, it's my job to sit here and entertain, it's their job to act interested. This Gayle, though: she's the first one to get the smartmouth about it.

As if Marshall were any of her business.

I bet everybody has this whole private part of themself someplace inside, and I'm no different. I've got my secrets and my wishes and my dreams. None of that is anyone's business. Still: that's what these people want. They want to open you up like a frog in biology and look around. They'd be in there picking up your heart, lifting up your guts. "Ah, hah! Looky here! This boy is nuts. He's got a dirty mind, too. See, that's all he thinks about all the time."

1. As if you don't, too.

2. As if it were any of your concern what I think about.

Do yourself a favor: keep the personal crap to yourself.

Still: Old Gayle's sitting there raising her eyebrows waiting for me to spill.

I shrug my shoulders hoping she'll lose interest.

"Tell you what I'll do," she says. "I'll ask some questions and all you have to do is answer them."

I decide to play along.

"What's your favorite food?"

"Pizza."

"Do you like your school?"

"It sucks."

"See how easy this is? Let's see—let's try a standard: What do you want to be when you grow up?"

An adult?

"I haven't given it much thought," I say.

Gayle tells me I should give it thought. Tells me to tell her when I do know.

"You can spend your whole life floundering if you're not careful. Not that you have to do just one thing. You just have to do some thing. Something you care about, something worthwhile."

I promise her I'd think about it.

She gets herself some Red Zinger tea, and comes back and puts her arm behind my back.

"We're ready for the tough ones now," she says. "You ready?"

"Not really," I say.

"Here we go: What do you value most—what's the most important thing in the world to you?"

"I'm not sure I understand. Maybe it's friends?"

"Don't ask me," Gayle says. "And don't be so vague. If that's what you mean, then say it like you mean it. Say friends are the most important thing to me."

Gayle goes on:

"Folks need to say what they need to say. You shouldn't be afraid of what people think. Especially if it's your own opinion. There's all these people out there who try to make up the rules on what gets said, how it gets said, who says it. That's how they keep quiet the people they didn't want to hear from."

"What do you care about?" I ask her.

"Our people. Most of all. More than anything else." Then she asks the real big one.

"Do you miss your mother?" she asks. Then she says, "Now, this time, what you do is — you tell me to mind my own damn business. You don't have to answer everything, you know."

She doesn't know me too well.

I tell her no. "I don't miss her at all."

"A very direct answer," she says. "Though I think an unfortunate one."

I look at her while I think of what to say. If anything. She's a tiny person, smaller than me, really. Brownskin. An Afro. There's something open about her face. A face you'd hate to have. Not because it's homely — it's not. But because I bet you could never hide how you felt.

I can tell, for example, she is sad that I don't miss Rose. Her face also tells me that it's my choice. Strangely, that makes me think it over.

Do I miss Rose?

"We weren't getting along too good." I tell her. She asks me why. Talking to Gayle, looking at Gayle — it's so easy. Just then I have a realization: it was never like this with Rose. With her it was always like just before a storm. You checked every word, never looked too close. One false move and there would be an explosion. Before I can stop, I say the terrible thing.

"We didn't like each other too much, my mother and me."

"But you love each other. I know how that is. It's a very sad thing."

"Don't feel bad about my mother. She made her choice."

"No question — she jacked ya'll up real good. I'm sad for you, though. It's sad when people hurt you so much."

"I'm just fine," I say. "Sam and I both are. It's like she was never here."

"It's not that easy, my friend."

I lower my head and don't look at Gayle. I've said too much.

Damn her, she pried right in.

She pats my arm and says, "Well, maybe sometimes it is that easy." She does that in a way that is surprising and calming. For once I sit still and I know that there is nothing I need to say.

*

Just so, here comes the next letter from Rose:

Son,

Wish this was a letter to tell you I'd gone over the rainbow. Wish I had big news.

I work and I work and then I work some more. I get pinched and patted on the behind. I laugh with the girls when we count our tiny tips. We're too tired to talk about much of anything except how tired we are.

I share a tiny place with two others. I work and I sleep. That's all.

Oh, and I think. About me and about you. And Sam.

You know me. I am the way I am.

And how's that?

Most important, I can take care of my own self. Do what I want. Be as tired and as lonely as anyone else. And stupid. But, at least I'm in charge of it. I wonder did I travel all this way just to find that out.

You the other thing I was ever in charge of. I know that now, too. Sam was so busy being the best trash man west of the Mississippi. So Marshall Field Finney was my little project. I made you the way you are. Bet you don't want to be hearing that.

Listen, one time I had taken you shopping up to Northwest Plaza. Back when it was still new. You were just a little thing. We were outside that Woolworth's and heading across to what used to be Vandervorts and Scruggs. A white woman stopped and patted you on the head.

"Isn't he a cute little thing," she said. One of those scrawny old white ladies, and I told her to watch where she put her damn hands. I pulled you to me and told her she best move herself on. Acting like she ain't never seen a black child before. I told her we was all cute, every damn one of us.

I looked down at you and you got that scrunched up rat-faced look on your face. We stalked off, almost ran. Had us a good laugh, too.

Remember that. Remember all the times like that. Right afterwards I bought you a strawberry cone at the Baskin Robbins. Do you remember that?

I decided early I wanted you to be as hard as nails. Not a paper cut-out

*doll like me. Stubborn. Tough-minded. I told off teachers at parent con-
ferences right in front of you. I made you throw books in the librarian's
face. If they got that tone with us. Like we was dirt.*

*"Don't move," I told you. "Don't move until they do it the way you want
it done." Take nothing off of no one. Live proud.*

*And when you turned into what I wanted to be . . . When it was too
late . . . When you were already Sam's boy . . . When there was nothing
left for me . . .*

*You know, I'd do it all again, too. Build that wall between us. I don't
have one regret. I know at least you'll never be running off to a place like
this. A place that's all plastic and cardboard. Painted and fancied-up with
lights, but then underneath is a place just like everyplace else. Like
Washington Park.*

A crackerbox is a crackerbox.

*That song is on the radio now. "Ain't No Mountain High Enough." If
you need me, call me, it says.*

I don't expect you will. And that makes me sort of happy.

Mother

*

Poor Rose: she'd completely lost it.

I stash the letter with the others—in there with the pictures of
Czechoslovakia, of cyclones. In Rose's encyclopedias. Her genius books.
The books she bought—Sam bought—so that "little Marshall would
have an advantage at school." The books for which every year she orders
the yearbook that updates it: '82, '83, '84, '85, '86. She waits for it by
the mailbox and unwraps it like a present. She wedges it in there with
the rest of them until they explode from the shelves. "A," and '85 and
'86 have to rest on their sides on the top. The only books she owns
whose main characters don't have guns or one syllable names like Mick
or Duke or Tack.

"Use them," she orders, her finger pointed. "Use them."

I'm using them now.

*

Sam and I have dinner alone for the first time in a while. Gayle has
to work late at her clinic. We fry up in a skillet a whole bunch of greasy
hamburgers and onions. I put a couple of slices of cheese on each of

mine, but Sam likes his plain with a lot of salt and a little mustard. We eat Kass BarBQ potato chips right from the bag, pass it back and forth between us.

Sam gets hot about this story on the news.

"What do they need to build some damn football stadium out in the county for. Too much damn traffic on 70 as it is."

"Must be some money in it someplace," I say.

"There you go — now you're talkin. You see one of these big deals and you know there's got to be some money in it for somebody. Pass them chips over here."

I do, and he crunches some down

After the news Sam gets up to help me with the dishes. I wash, he scrubs the sink and counters and puts the dishes away.

"I got a letter from my mother," I tell him. "A couple actually." I'd never told him about any of the others. I'm not looking at him but I hear him stop what he's doing, if only for a second.

"Good girl," he says. "Glad she doing right by you." He doesn't ask what the letter says or anything. Never once has he said anything about her at all. We finish the dishes in silence.

Back at the TV Sam sets the VCR. He's taping a show on PBS — one of those opera deals, this one with a big fat black lady just singing her lungs out.

"Gayle asked me to get this for her," he says. "We can watch something else if you want. Damn if I'm gonna sit through this here twice."

We watch basketball on cable. "What do you think of Gayle?" he asks me.

I tell him she seems like a good person — real friendly.

Sam says, "Sho nuff is." Says he could get used to having her around full time.

*

In my room that night I listen to the radio in the dark.

Sam and Rose.

Sam and Gayle.

It's easy as changing bags in the garbage can.

I think about what Sam says about Rose doing right by me.

So there: as easily rid as Sam is, me, I'll have Rose the rest of my life, doing the right thing.

On the radio Tina Turner sings "Let's Stay Together."
"I'm so in love with you . . ."
Into my head comes another voice. There's a duet going on.
". . . whether times are good or bad, happy or sad."
I know that other voice. It's Rose.
Who'd guess she'd be as good as Tina?

13

APRIL FIRST.

As we gather on the back field close to the railroad right-of-way, the Pinheads are in high spirits. It is almost the perfect spring day, sunny and warm, everything shimmering and yellow-green.

I'll be damn:

Todd and Ohairy have pulled it off, somehow gotten the Pinheads interested, even excited about something.

I'd expected they'd be here only out of curiosity, that there'd be a lot of standing around with arms crossed, watching. But everyone has gotten off into this, wearing their brightest day-glo colors, tossing frisbees, footballs . . . Some girls are jumping ropes and singing, pretending they are little girls. There's Connie Jo wearing what looks like a witch's dress, all black, shredded and flowing. A mob of kids — rockers and punks — are dancing out in the middle of the field, ten boxes turned to ten different stations.

Artie and his little friend Susan are right in the middle of that dancing mob out there. They're always together, those two. Miss Ida and probably Betty Lou, too, would die — their Baby Boy with a white girl. People here at Eisenhower figure it's okay as long as they're both . . . of limited abilities, special. Or, at least pretend like they don't care.

You see black boys and white girls together sometimes out at the mall, but hardly ever white boys with black girls. Most of us — black or white — wouldn't do it anyway. But especially the boys. I think that's because if you are a boy you always have to worry about what your dad thinks, how he's gonna act around her. Dad's are always telling you about looking out for yourself. For your future. If I brought a white girl to the crackerbox, old Sam wouldn't say nothing to her face. He'd look her up and down real good, though, and then, afterwards he'd say, "You must got the white girl fever. What you want with a skinny butt little gal like that anyway?" Old Sam is always talking about how white folks ain't got no behinds. And, as much as I hate to say it, and not that I go around looking at a lot of white people's behinds, Sam may be right.

Personally, if Arthur Warner wants to run around with this Susan, hey, it's fine with me. Though I have to ask myself how it is someone like him could find a girlfriend. What, do I have a giant cooties sign around my neck? I just hope they don't have a houseful of retarded kids.

Pretend I never said that.

Half the school must be out here for the demonstration. The other half we can see watching out the south windows.

There are even news cameras — little box-like jobs with station decals pasted all over. These deals are carried on the shoulders of a couple of guys with power packs strapped to their backs. I can see one of the cameras pointed up at us and I give them a big wave. Todd tells me to grow up.

Todd and I are at the top of the visiting team bleachers. We are watching down the tracks for the train. Todd will signal with a homemade air-raid siren when the train is near, signaling the Pinheads to put the fun in high gear, and also signaling the cameras to get ready for when everybody falls-out.

"Just look at those people down there," Todd says. "I didn't think it was possible, but I guess you can do anything. You just have to try." His eyes are practically brimmed over with tears. To their credit he and Miss O'Hare planned this down to the last detail. They kept all the talking stuff to a minimum. Todd made one little presentation. People actually showed up for it. He wrote one article for the newspaper. He talked mostly about what we don't know about this nuclear stuff and, also, how citizen involvement makes important people take notice. What Todd and Ohairy did most and best was to emphasize the fun.

Just like I told them to. I mean, one thing a Pinhead likes is to have a good time.

Down there looks like we'd won a state championship or canceled school forever.

*

High noon finds Todd staring down the tracks.

"Come on," he says, clutching tight at the binoculars. Down on the field the Pinheads are running out of steam. Here and there clusters of kids have sat down to enjoy the sun. Artie and Susan and some of their friends are still working out, though. Todd looks around. He's so nervous he's rubbed a spot raw on his elbow from clutching it with the opposite hand.

I tell him to relax. "Trains are always a little late," I say. "We'll have time to get them up and going as soon as you see it."

Across the way on the rise by the parking lot I can see Mr. Shannon checking his watch. Fourth period begins in less than ten minutes. Already some kids are wandering back to the building.

Some guy we've never seen before is hanging out up there next to O'Hare. She's been standing up with the faculty. Here she comes strutting across the field to the bottom of the bleachers, calling Todd down. "Take over," he says. He hands me the binoculars and goes down to see what she wants.

About a dozen or so of their hard core supporters come over and join them. Like Todd, they are real serious. They all scowl a lot and wear the same buttons. If you could save the ozone layer wearing buttons we'd be in good shape with this crowd alone. Some of the boys down there have even taken the Lawrence fashion cue – old vests, buttoned-down shirts, jeans and all. Strange to me, though, they don't try to hang around with Todd and Artie and me, and though I might as well be invisible, they treat Todd as if he were the president and Jesus all rolled into one skinny package – real deferential, almost as if they thought he had super powers.

O'Hare finishes with Todd and and pats him on the arm. Then I see him turn to his troops. He is, I can tell, giving them new orders of some kind.

"What's the story?" I ask when he returns.

"Everything's under control," he says.

At 12:10 Mr. Shannon raises a bullhorn. He says, "Let's go, people." Through the bullhorn his voice sounds especially twangy and nasal.

In clusters the Pinheads wander back across the field. I pick up the rigged-up siren and say, "I guess that's that."

Todd grabs my arm. "We're staying." he says. He keeps the binoculars stuck to his eyes, staring down the tracks. Down on the field all but about twenty kids have gone. The hard core recruits line up along the right-of-way.

Artie and Susan run over to the bottom of the bleachers. "Come on you guys," Artie yells. "Everybody's already gone."

"You go on in," Todd says, all sure of himself and smooth. You'd think he were giving somebody permission to do something.

Artie and Susan wave these big smiley waves and run in. They are the last two who will leave. Ohairy turns and follows them into the building.

"So it's okay for Artie to go, but I get to stay," I say.

Todd lowers the binoculars from his eyes and gives me about the hardest look I've ever seen on him. He doesn't say anything but I know he's daring me to go, daring me to chicken-out and not stand with him.

What I don't know just then is that O'Hare has struck some sort of a deal with Shannon so that Todd and company can stay. They — we — are to suffer only the minimum consequence, and the school will still have gone on record making a statement.

Kind of a shrewd deal, I guess, but what I really think when I find out is, I wonder how often it is that these deals go on. I mean, it just could be that every time you think something sort of tough is about to go on, behind it there's some sort of a cheesy deal. Don't you just know it's true. When you look at those politicians on TV, can't you just tell that half of them are running a scam. Scratch my back, and I'll scratch yours. That's how Sam says it goes. Out there in the big world. You got to give to get. Great, but what if you don't want to give. What if the price is too high. I can hear that Sam up there in the dump, dickering and dealing. Take these aluminum cans and I'll throw in that scrap iron for free. I'll move your fridge if you come on a date. Is that what O'Hare and Todd did? Is that the kind of person I'm dealing with now?

"I see you're still here," Todd says to me. He says it as a simple statement. Nothing nasty intended. At least I don't think there is.

I just sit there on the bleachers looking out in the day, thinking to myself, "Oh, shit."

*

At 12:34 Todd says "here she comes" and I hit the air raid siren. We quick meet the others at the fence and join hands. The train approaches – a short train, only four cars counting an engine. As the cars pass we all die dramatic deaths. I gasp and choke and shake. Todd tells me to give it a rest. Up in the windows I can hear Pinheads screaming and cheering.

I feel foolish and proud at the same time.

*

Despite pats on the back we are herded into the office for the official reading of the riot act. We are told that the demonstration was a success, and that we have managed to focus attention on an important issue in a positive way. We "are to be congratulated." Then we are told that because, technically speaking, we have violated school rules, we have to be made to suffer the consequences. That's just how it sounds, too – all official and off, as if old Shannon was reading it right out of the official rules book, which he was.

The consequences: two afternoons of school service.

Mr. Shannon adds, "We have, of course, already notified your parents."

Crap.

Before I can catch Todd's reaction to that, Mr. Shannon calls him aside. "I want you to meet one of our former Eisenhower students. Mr. Mark Randall. He's here to get some pictures of y'all."

They shake hands and Todd tells him his name. This is a tall blond guy with a bushy moustache – the same guy I saw standing up on the hill by Ohairy. He tells Todd, "Good show today." He says it was real professional. He's wearing one of those Todd outfits, too.

O'Hare stands back out of the scene. She's looking back and forth between the two of them. She's got a tight little smile on her face. Like the vampire got in the blood bank.

Shannon says, "Todd reminds me a lot of you back in those days. Always cooking something up." Shannon laughs a throaty laugh that sounds like he's gulping air.

Mark Randall and Todd sneer at him behind his back.

132

I just roll my eyes.

Randall and Todd sit down to talk about "things." Todd is so involved I bet he forgot all about the forged note.

*

"Here comes the Black Panther himself," Sam says when I come home.

Me and one of Todd's lieutenants have just spent two hours stapling school discipline manuals—we must have stapled thirty years' worth. I switched pages six and eight on about half of them. This dude I worked with was—if you believe it—more serious than Todd. Kept talking about the movement this, the movement that. I asked him what movement, a bowel movement? and after that he wouldn't talk to me at all.

Gayle and Sam think that Marshall in the principal's office is the funniest thing they've heard since television was invented.

"Them white folks didn't scare my little fella?" Sam asks.

I give him a dirty look, which makes Gayle say something about the life of a black militant not leaving any time for funny business. They can hardly contain themselves, they are laughing so hard.

If Rose were here who knows what she'd do. When I was in trouble, sometimes she would act almost like she was proud of it. Sometimes it was like she didn't care, but that wasn't really it. It was more like she was sorry that it wasn't her who was in trouble instead of me.

Sam and Gayle are enjoying this more than she ever would. They even think it's funny that I forged Rose's signature to the fake note.

I put on some dark sunglasses and try to look real mean. If you can't beat 'em join 'em. Sam and Gayle laugh even harder. The laughter continues into dinner and even after.

"Now, Mr. Sam," Gayle says. "Do you think this is any way to bring up a child. No respect for the law. An outlaw. That's what you're raising. A regular Jesse James."

We are sitting around the TV set, but the set's not on. That never happened in the old days, either.

"You absolutely right, Miss Gayle," Sam says. "It ain't fittin. It just ain't fittin." Then he stands over me. "Shame on you, boy. Shame on you." He waves a finger in my direction.

By this time I'm laughing so hard at them myself my sides start to ache.

"I'll be good," I say. "I promise forever to be good."

"Are you gonna have to kill him?" Gayle asks.

"He's been a good little fella up to now. I think I'll let him off this time."

"Oh thank you, thank you," I say. I crawl over and wrap my arms around the bottoms of Sam's legs. "I'll be good forever and ever."

"Don't let him off that easy," Gayle says. "Make him do something. Make him get us some ice water."

"You heard the lady. Two ice waters and make it damn quick." Then Sam says to her, "You one of them smart girls, ain't you?" He nudges her arm. "We may just have to keep you around here."

"Aren't you sweet," Gayle says. "Don't ever call me a girl again." She hits him on the arm with a pillow. They both laugh some more at that.

This sort of stuff's been going on all evening. I move out to get the water, partially because Sam and Gayle are kinda sickening sometimes, and partially because Sam lightly kicks my butt and says, "Thirsty folks get tired of waiting."

They toast with the ice water as if it were champagne.

"Now. You tell us about your checkered past, Mr. Sam," Gayle orders.

"I'd hate to upset a sweet young thing like you. What are you, sixteen? seventeen?"

"How did you guess?" Gayle asks.

Gayle is Sam's age — thirty-nine. She told me she was. She goes, "I think my tender ears can handle it. Marshall and I want to hear all about your militant days."

"My daddy didn't allow none of that," Sam says.

We laugh. We think he's still messing around.

"No, listen, this is for real," he says.

So we listen.

"Out here they was some of them old-fashioned Negroes. They didn't take no stuff from white folks, mind you. But all that civil rights stuff . . ."

"No picket lines in Washington Park," Gayle says.

"My daddy would see Dr. King on television and he'd say that there was one smart Negro boy. He'd also say he thought a lot of folks was gonna end up gettin hurt."

"What did you think?" I ask.

"I thought maybe I might like to join one of those demonstrations. But didn't no demonstration come my way."

"And you didn't go out looking for none," Gayle says.

"That's right. Yes, ma'am," Sam says. "I'm glad all that went on. Proud. I'm just saying it seemed like it just passed me right by."

Gayle says, "We had some action at my high school. We took over the guidance office. I was sick of all the bullshit—you know. How if you're black or poor they automatically put you in the vocational track. They still on that these days?" she asks me.

"At Eisenhower they're too busy trying to be nice."

"As if you was made out of glass."

"Or not there at all," I say.

"We made sure they saw us," Gayle goes on. "Real well-organized. We wrote up concerns, ideas, suggestions. Then we had a sit-in. They treated us like dogs. They dragged folks out of there by whatever they could grab—belts, hair. Kicked me all up in my legs. Called us niggers and bitches. I'll never forget that as long as I live."

Sam takes her hand and holds it between two of his. Her hand fits between those two mits almost like a cat's paw would.

I ask her if it was worth it. She puts her head on Sam's shoulder. Sam says it was.

*

When the doorbell rings I get up to get it. Lucille pushes in without so much as a hello, grabs me by the collar and hauls me in front of Sam and Gayle as if before judge and jury. Getting an eyeful of how cozy they are knocks a little of the wind from her sails. She shakes the collar around a bit. Almost, but not quite rough, is how she's acting.

"I caught the six o'clock news," Lucille says. "Y'all catch the news? Or were you too busy?"

"Get your hands off my boy," Sam says. He says it mildly, at least for him. He says, "And good evening to you, too, Miss Robinson."

Lucille drops the collar. I start laughing because I can see Gayle biting her lip. That causes Lucille to grab the collar again.

"I'm disappointed, Sam Finney. Awful disappointed."

"This is my wife's aunt. Gayle, Lucille. Lucille, Gayle."

Lucille has obviously left her house in a hurry. She's pulled on some sort of red, black, and green knit cap over her hair—one that does not quite hide the mass of curlers. She's got on a house dress with big red and yellow flowers on it. And that purse—the gigantic, day-glo blue purse — she's got that hung on the hinge of her elbow. If she hits me with that monster I'll be crippled for life.

"I'm having my dinner," she says. "On the TV I see one of my own flesh and blood. Bigger than life. Waving and grinning like a Chessy cat. I thought the Lord Jesus would take me home right then and there."

Hot damn — one of those cameras actually caught us. And here we are having so much fun we forget to watch.

"Do you want something, Lucille?" Sam asks.

I laugh and she squeezes tighter at the collar. I'm standing on tiptoes because she's pulling up it too.

"I want this foolishness stopped. This family don't go in for no public carrying on. Your people neither, Sam Finney. I want you to do something about this."

"What am I gonna do if some mostly grown nigger wants to get himself in a little trouble? You got a hold of him — you talk to him."

Lucille drops me. She points a finger right at Sam, tilts her head in Gayle's direction. "I see you're at it again. You old dog. Ain't nothing but a dog, and I'm warning you. I don't like what's going on here one bit. I won't stand for it." She turns on Gayle who is still biting her lip. "What are you looking at, girl?"

Gayle purses her lips and shakes her head.

"Tell me and we'll both know," she says.

Sam laughs right out loud.

"I'll take care of you," Lucille says to Sam. Then to me she says, "You know better than to mess with me." She turns and slams the door behind her.

"That is related to you?" Gayle asks me.

"Flesh and blood," I say. "What do you think she's gonna do?" I ask Sam.

"Not much she can do," he says. "She'll call Rose."

"That doesn't bother you?" I ask

"I'll tell Rose myself. Next time I talk to her." Sam says this as if it was the most ordinary thing in the world.

"You talk to ma?"

"Every so often, sure."

No reaction from Gayle, so I guess I'm the only one surprised by this.

*

Staring at the ceiling that night, I find the hole and let myself be taken in. It's like I have X-ray vision and I can dissolve through, right through the gravel, right through the roof, out above the house, out into space. I stare and let my mind go out there where it can wander free.

But it won't go anywhere. It stays right here in the middle of all this. Hashing it over, working it out.

It goes back and forth from how sweet Sam had treated Gayle, to the fact that Rose has been in touch with him.

Which means she won't leave him alone either.

I decide what she is doing is keeping her options open. Maybe nothing better'll come along. She's like a giant shadow over all our lives, Rose is. And I get some comfort, strangely enough, knowing Sam has to deal with that just as much as I do.

*

In the morning I find out the shadow over Sam and me might not be the worst thing in the world. Todd shows up at Miss Ida's with a black eye. A swollen handprint on his left cheek glows brighter than the morning sun.

14

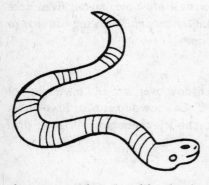

"WHAT HAPPENED TO you?" I ask. Artie and I are waiting for him in the store. Miss Ida puts down the puzzle page and her coffee mug. She comes around the counter.

"Let me see," she says. She moves his head around taking a good look at the evidence by gripping his chin and doing what she wants with it. Just like the dentist does.

"I ran into a door," Todd says. His tone is bitter, and even a bit evil. He looks Miss Ida right in the eye when he says this.

She turns loose the chin. Her eyes meet mine briefly as she turns back to the counter. Her face is almost blank, but her eyes show how she feels: angry and helpless.

"Pretty big hand on that door. You want something to put on that?" she offers.

"No," Todd says. "Thanks for asking."

"I got some sunglasses you can use," says Artie.

"If I wanted sunglasses I'd be wearing sunglasses."

*

All the way to school no one says anything more.

"Hang on a second," I say. We are walking from the parking lot to the building. "You look pretty bad. You sure you're up to this?"

"What I look like is, I look like someone beat the shit out of me."

"People will stare at you," I tell him.

"I got nothing to hide," he says. "I didn't do anything."

He strolls into Eisenhower High School bigger than life, staring down the stares, wearing those bruises as if they were badges.

*

I get out of study hall and go knock on Miss O'Hare's door during study hall. It is standing slightly open. As I knock I push the door just a bit, expecting to see Todd. Instead I see Ohairy with her arms around the waist of Blondie, the dude from the demonstration. He's got his hands on her shoulders.

"That's the way — come right on in Marshall," Ohairy says, neither embarassed nor even angry. She introduces me as one of her "advisees," and old Mark Randall gives me one of these old-fashioned soul handshakes that some white folks are always trying to do. As if it made them something special because they were in on a big secret. I turn my hand every which way pretending like I don't have the slightest idea what he's doing.

"I saw you at the demonstration," Mark says to me. "Great job."

"Mark and I are old friends," Ohairy tells me.

That's obvious.

"From our college radical days — the good old days."

Who cares?

"Can I help you with something?" she asks me.

I say "Yes." I give old straw head the evil eye. Randall takes the cue, and Ohairy promises to call him later. When he leaves I close the door behind him.

I ask her if she'd seen Todd today.

"We talked after second hour," she says. "Yesterday was such a success. We're planning something new already. Such momentum."

"What about Todd's face?"

"What's the story there? It looks awful. I hope he put something on it."

"Todd got the hell beat out of him."

"I'm surprised to hear about our Todd in a fight," she says. "He's certainly not the fighting type."

"His dad did it."

"Oh." She covers her mouth and starts chewing her finger. "Did he tell you that?"

"Todd says he walked into a door," I say. "Does it look like he walked into a door to you? I think his dad beat him up after you made him be in the demonstration."

"Well, first of all, I never *made* Todd do anything." Ohairy, who's been leaning on her desk, sits down in her chair. She raises a hand as if to stop me from speaking. She snickers and shakes her head. "There's one thing I'm starting to figure out finally. You give me too much power. You don't give enough credit to Todd."

"What I know is that Todd is really gullible. And now he's hurt. How are you going to help him?"

"I'm not sure what I can do. Oh, Marshall, this is so awful. Poor Todd."

"What about those people who did this to him?"

"Abuse is a very serious charge, Marshall."

"You didn't even look at him. He walks in here with a black eye and you don't even see it." I'm yelling this at her. "You don't care about Todd at all."

"I care very, very, much. People like Todd are rare. You're right. I wasn't thinking. We were so excited."

I roll my eyes at her.

"You know, I saw that eye right away. I really did. But we started carrying on about yesterday. And I guess I just . . . slipped. Can you forgive me?"

I get up and head for the door.

"Please, sit down and listen to me."

I refuse.

"Then just listen," she says.

Ohairy tells me that if it's true, she should report it, but she's worried. That could make it worse for Todd. If it's not true and she reports it, it could ruin his family. She says she could call just on the suspicion. She's doing all this thinking out loud. She decides maybe it's best to let it be for now. She says she's going to keep a close eye on Todd.

I don't buy any of it. I start out the door.

"Beaten is beaten," I say. Whatever is supposed to happen to that trash should happen to them.

"This is very personal stuff, Marshall," Ohairy says. "We have to trust him. He'll let us know if and when he needs us."

I give her a dirty look and leave.

Ohairy is not to be trusted. I've known that all along. She's too good at turning stuff around, at making apples sound like oranges. People like her need to be fixed, and fixed good. But, she's the teacher. The adult. She holds all the cards. Somebody get me a gun. I am not totally helpless. I got my mouth, and I can save Todd. I can save him from those people and from Ohairy, too. I'll worry about getting him away from her later. For now, I go to the pay phone in the main hall by the office and ask who to talk to about child abuse. I tell them I want something done about it. Now.

*

After school Gayle asks me to go walking with her. We walk up Dorset toward the landfill. There is a big sign on Dorset by the entrance that says "Desperate for clean dirt."

Just like Saint Louis in the spring, today is cool, almost cold because the wind blows just a little. The sky is full of raggedy gray and white clouds. Here and there a bright patch of blue flashes through.

Gayle's got on a bulky white sweater with big wooden buttons. It looks much too big for her. I have to stick my hands in the kangaroo pockets of my sweatshirt to keep them warm. We see Sam but don't go bother him. He's directing some men who have dumptrucks full of black earth. Since last summer the dump is mostly filled. Sam spends his days salvaging whatever is left here that might be worth anything. Who knows what the dirt is for.

We wave at Sam and he does this real obnoxious thing where he waves, grins, and sticks up two thumbs.

"What's his problem?" I ask.

"Loves life," Gayle says. "Come on up here."

We walk over to one of the high places—an old pile of gravel that never got sold and is now mixed with dirt. The boys and I called that hill the Matterhorn. Now the land has filled in around the old mountain. It's hardly even a good hill anymore, though you can still see most of Washington Park from here.

Up there, this is the question I ask Gayle:

I ask her what would you do if your parents beat you up—abused you and all of that.

"Did they do that to you?" she asks.

I walked right into that one.

I deny it up and down, hoping she's convinced. I tell her it's one of those just supposing questions.

She says they call them hypothetical questions – which I knew, but didn't feel like using a fancy word. She says she doesn't believe in hypothetical questions.

"I love people. All of their what if this and what if that bullshit. As if life were some kind of a fairy tale and you could make up endings to suit you. People might really want to talk about stuff too, but either they shamed or else they really don't want to hear what you have to say. I don't have time in my life for either of those. Which is it with you?"

"With me it's that I don't think I should be spreading other people's business around."

"Then don't," she says. She turns toward the dump trucks which are roaring around at one edge of the landfill.

"But I do want to know what you think."

Gayle gives me an annoyed look, frowning out from under these drawn-on eyebrows.

"Todd's parent's slapped him around last night. He was beat up pretty good. Probably cause of the demonstration."

She parts her lips, makes a clicking sound. She touches me on the arm. That's all.

"What do you think?" I ask her.

"It's a pretty cold thing to do. I'm sorry it happened."

I'm getting the feeling that this is something folks don't want to know about. I doubt they'd be so cool if they had the shit beat out of them. She and O'Hairy both: sighing, shaking their heads. That makes me sick. People like them pretend to be open and honest. And maybe they are. But they've got their closed parts, too. Every once in awhile you come up against those closed doors, and then just watch 'em flinch. It's always stuff like this that gets em: people who are two-faced, people who hit their kids. They're afraid of that stuff. Afraid that if they talk about it maybe, somehow, it'll get them, too.

"Aren't there laws?" I ask her. "Shouldn't somebody do something?"

"Do what?" she asks. "Your friend's what . . . sixteen? Not exactly what I call helpless."

From the rise we can see the trucks emptying out their loads of soil. A man in red coveralls walks behind a truck, spreading the dirt with a rake. In the cool air the dirt smells rich, like summer. Sam stands on a hill across the dump. His legs are spread and his arms are crossed like an ancient chieftain.

"I can't get it out of my head," I say. "I don't understand how you could do that to your own child."

"Life do get tough," Gayle says. "Everyday at the clinic I see kids coming in that are beaten. There are a lot of sick people out there. When I get to be queen . . ." She lets out a little laugh. But, for now . . ." she shrugs her shoulders. "It's just another one of those things."

"But if you loved someone . . ."

"Love," Gayle laughs. "Well, now, little brother, you have really stirred things up. Tell me all about this love. Go on."

I just shake my head.

"I'll tell you, then. First, just because you got a child don't mean you have to love it. Even if you do," she's moving her hands a lot, walking me down by the fence that separates the park from the dump. "Even if you do, sometimes when you love somebody you have to do something that hurts them."

I tell her that that sounds stupid. That people who love should only do good things to each other.

"Well, aren't you sweet," she says, batting her eyes. "Let's say we're walking in this dump and you step on a shard of glass. Let's say it got in your foot. Though it might hurt you, I'd sure pull it out. I'd put some of that good stinging disinfectant on it also."

"That's not the same thing," I say.

She rubs her chin as if she were searching hard for another, better example. "Okay — your mama. Just listen." She grabs my arm as I walk away from her, repelling her with my hands. "I think she left," she says, pulling me back around to her, "because she was messed up and she was afraid of what she might do. She hurt you in one way to keep from hurting you in another way. That's just my opinion from all that Sam tells me about her. Just think about it."

Not that I would say anything more about Rose to her anyway.

*

Just as we are about to leave Sam yells at us, tells us to come back. He says he's got great news. He is standing by the shed with his thumbs hitched up in his overalls, rocking on his heels, looking for all the world like a big black country bumpkin.

"Step into my office," he says, as if he were really the mayor of Washington Park. Inside the lean-to Sam has nailed up the license plates from every junked car that ever had one. There is a desk — it's really an old flat door set on top of two file cabinets — and it is now clean (or at least not real messy like it was getting for a while there). Above the desk there is a picture of a black woman with big boobs and a small bikini. Apparently she is Miss April at the Icehouse Lounge. Her name is Dawnette. I can't help staring.

"What are you looking at?" Sam says. He hands me a Dixie cup with some grape juice in it. It looks as if we're about to have some sort of a toast.

"Ladies and gentlemen," he begins.

Yes, definitely a toast.

"Thanks to a certain Miss Gayle Moore, myself, Mr. Samuel Finney, Jr., has taken this here contract to one of them fancy lawyers over in Clayton for a little reviewing."

"I was right," Gayle shouts. "I knew I was right."

"Hush and just hang on — big old horsey girl. Don't spill none of that juice here in my fancy suite."

Sam drinks his juice, so Gayle and I do the same. He refills us from the Hi-C can.

"Save it for the toast," he says. "As I was saying, upon consultation with my attorneys, it appears those old county boys done my daddy a bit of a favor some time back."

Sam keeps looking at me and I think his eyes are about to pop out of his head.

"Let me back up," he says. "My daddy . . . was a good man. A giant. A saint. Don't nobody say nothing against that man. That clear?"

We agree, toast, and drink down some more juice. Sam fills us up again.

"Hold off on my drink. We gonna have us a toast. A giant of a man, but ignorant . . ." Sam emphasizes each syllable of ignorant. "Daddy must not have had one day of education. He could read, but if the paper said the price of milk went up, daddy'd say there was a shortage of eggs."

"Get to the point," Gayle says. She's jumping up and down, pulling at Sam's sleeve.

"Come and read," he says. He gathers us at his side as if he were the mother hen and we were his baby chicks.

"Read it," he orders me, his arm across my shoulder. "Start right here."

I read where he points. "It says: 'said use shall last into perpetuity or until capacity, at which time deed shall revert to original owner-ship or duly appointed heirs thereof.'"

"You understand?" he asks. "It is ours—the landfill is. Yours and mine, son."

"That lawyer was absolutely sure?" Gayle asks.

"Not one doubt. Ours. As soon as the land is back the way it was—that's what the dirt is for."

Sam raises his cup. "This grape juice'll have to do. But we'll have us a big celebration soon. For now, one big glass all around. To all of us," he says. We drink up.

Then he puts his big hands on Gayle's shoulders. "My thanks to you," he says. "I never would have thought to look at that contract. I about gave up on everything. Now me and this boy right here, we got something to look forward to."

Sam gives Gayle one of those long kisses just like in the movies. She lays her head contentedly on his chest. Sam looks at me as if I were made out of gold.

*

I leave Gayle at the shed with Sam.

Walking back home I give all of this some thought.

I'd asked Sam did this mean we were rich now or something. He acted as if that were the least important thing on earth.

But, after all, what has really gone on here, anyway? He finally read the damn contract. That's all. He found out about something he ought to have known all along. And where was he anyway? Just not paying attention as usual. It's like Dorothy in the movie who finds out she only has to click her heels to go home, that happiness is right in her own back yard. Me, I'd have gone upside that witch's head for putting me through all that broomstick crap. Still, somehow, for Sam, this bit about his deed is bigger. Which means something else is going on here, too. I mean, what sort of a moral is "remember to read the fine print."

The other thing I think about is what Gayle says about love. Like a lot of what all of them say, it sounds like garbage when you play it back in your head. Then I remember the stuff about having to hurt somebody because you love them. She said she'd do it for me. I believe that. I believe she loves me the same way I love her. She may be Sam's age and Sam's gal. But she loves me too. I know it.

If that grape juice were wine I wouldn't have felt any better.

*

Sam feels so good he springs for carry-out Chinese. Very nutritious Gayle says. The egg rolls are soggy but the fried rice is full of shrimp and sweet onions. We eat right out of the cartons, passing them around the circle from one person to the next. You have to do that stuff sometimes: eat right out of the cartons. It's more fun and it gives you something else to think about besides dishes and table manners. Sam and Gayle poke pieces of shrimp into each other's mouths and giggle. Gayle spears her food with chopsticks. It almost looks like she is shoveling it in, but somehow she makes it look graceful. Sam takes careful plastic-forkfulls, always offering more to her and me. He pours the last few grains of rice in his mouth.

"Pig," Gayle teases.

There isn't one crumb left, so we crush the boxes and stuff them in the trash.

Sam decides to make a list of what he can do with his piece of land. He says everybody has to give him suggestions.

I suggest he sell it and make millions of dollars. Gayle says he should give it away to needy persons. Such as herself.

"Maybe I'll build a roller coaster," Sam says.

I get up to answer the knock at the door. I recognize it is Todd only because of the red hair. His other eye is blackened and blood trickles from both nostrils. A lot of blood has dripped to his white shirt. It also comes from the corner of his mouth.

Sam walks right over to him. He practically pushes me out of the way.

"Sit him down over here," Gayle says. She orders me to get her a washrag with some ice.

I do it.

I don't know what else to do.

Sam stands there rigid, clenching and unclenching his fists. "Who did this to you?" he asks.

Todd doesn't say anything. He moans a little as Gayle wipes around his face with the cloth. He is swollen. Some places on his face are purple.

"Where are your glasses?" I ask.

146

"I lost them," Todd says. It comes out cracked. He is trying hard not to cry.

"Who did it?" Sam demands.

I tell Sam that Todd's dad did it.

"That the truth?" Sam asks.

Todd nods feebly.

Though it seems like hours, it's just a minute before Sam decides what to do. He grabs his jacket and says, "Come on." He reaches down and wraps a big hand around Todd's arm. He gently helps him up.

"You come with me," Sam says.

They go to the door and I follow them out. Behind us Gayle looks stricken. She sits there on the couch holding the bloody wet cloth.

*

Sam stops the truck in front of the house down across the tracks. "This it?" he asks.

I tell him it is.

"Let's go," he says, but Todd balks. "Nothing is gonna happen. Just come on." Todd trembles as Sam guides him from the car.

"Just stay by me," Sam says.

The woman I'd seen before answers the door. She has the same long face as Todd, with mousey-colored hair, the head set on a large body. Not fat, but like a football player. When she sees us she calls out the name "Walt."

Bold Big Sam pushes right past her, into the living room, the tiny room with the faded yellow walls. Just the couch and the TV. There on one side of the room is the sewing machine. Around it are boxes of cloth. Some pieces are cut into squares and ovals. Another box is full of foam rubber pillows.

"Walt," the woman calls again. Todd quick goes over to the TV and picks up his glasses. It's almost as if they were set there deliberately on the TV stand, sitting next to a blue picture of Jesus.

Walt comes in from a back room. His blondish red hair is streaked with sweat. Tall and skinny. Like Todd. He's wiping grease off his hands with a paper towel.

"Can I do something for you, Finney?" he says, real cool.

"I come to find out what went on here," Sam says.

Walt gets a sneering smile on his face. "Last time I heard you were the county maintenance man."

"Did you hurt this boy?" Sam asks.

"That ain't none of your damn business."

I can tell Sam's getting hot. His lips are moving around as if he's trying to keep from saying something. Todd's mother is at her sewing machine. But she's just sitting there, just looking at it. Bright-colored pillows are scattered at her feet. They are out of place here, I think.

"No call for doing something like this," Sam says. "They got laws."

"I got laws in this house too. If he don't like it here, he can leave." Walt goes back to wherever again. Todd's mother is still frozen at the sewing machine. She bends her head over her work. She is doing nothing.

Sam sighs. He shakes his head. "You get your things," he orders Todd.

It doesn't take Todd five minutes to come back with a couple of sacks and an old backpack. As if he were the National Guard, ready to go at the drop of a hat. I grab the sacks.

Walt comes back around the corner.

"You leave outa here with those niggers and you don't come back."

Todd looks at his father for the first time since we came in — a cold, hard look. Then he walks out the door.

*

We set up a roll-away bed in my room and make it up for Todd.

"This can be your home," Sam says. "If you want."

Todd just lies down, clutching the backpack. In a few days he'll be just fine, but never really the same.

I go out and tell Sam "thanks."

"Young man caught a tough break," Sam says. "Okay with you that I put him in your room?"

As if I would object.

"You know how you are," he says, then he and Gayle have a good laugh.

"Marshall's snoring may run him out of here, too," Gayle adds.

More laughter. I wonder sometimes if they even know what's funny and what's not.

"What's going to happen to Todd?" I ask. "Is he gonna stay here forever?"

"See there," Sam says to Gayle. "Maybe it do bother him." They laugh some more, so I walk away.

"Look here," Sam says. "I mean what I say. Home is forever: my daddy taught me that. You don't turn away folks in need."

"What if they come after him?" I ask.

"Let em come," Sam shrugs.

Gayle makes a suggestion, "Todd ought to get himself freed from his parents — emancipated they call it."

"Whatever," Sam says. "It's that boy's life. We'll do what we can. You," he points to me, his voice almost fierce. "You go in there and make that boy welcome. I expect you to do right by me."

"Yes, sir," I say, and I decide at that very moment to do everything I can to be sure Todd is safe.

15

GAYLE HAS DECIDED it's time for driving lessons. Todd is off planning the revolution, and she says this is the perfect time to begin. She says two boys is more than even she can handle.

These days Todd has lost all interest in educating the Pinheads. Though he still runs class meetings, his heart's not in it.

Mark Randall and Todd are the team now. Where it used to be Kathy this and Kathy that, now I also have to hear what Blondie has to say about the world condition. Randall has convinced Todd that he's done all he can do at Eisenhower. Say's it's time for Todd to go on to other challenges.

"It means," Todd told me, "A bunch of apathetic suburban high school preppies are only going to do so much. It means getting in on the big action."

I told Todd that I didn't think there was a lot of big action going on out there these days, but he just said that I don't know everything. Evidently Randall does, and he tells Todd about all kinds of radical stuff going down – a lot of stuff that doesn't get into the papers cause "they" don't want people to know about it.

"Sure," I say.

Todd says that "Big Stuff" is going down soon and he wants to be right in the middle of the action. He says I'd better decide whether I'm in or out.

And off he goes to another meeting in the city. He says he'll fill me in when he gets back.

Gayle and I go driving.

I expect driving'll be easy because of having watched Artie do it. Of course, Artie would never allow anyone to touch Dentyne, and recently he's too busy sneaking around with Susan to bother teaching us. For just a minute it occurs to me that driving lessons are really Sam's job, and I tell Gayle that.

"Do you really want Sam Finney next to you while you're learning to drive?"

She's right: I might not live through lesson one.

Furthermore: she wants my new skill to be a big surprise for Sam.

Gayle drives a Toyota—an old one, a Tercel, but she keeps it clean.

She says to me, "The first thing is: if you're the driver you need to get in on the other side of the car."

Oh.

"Don't be nervous," she says. "This is the easiest, most natural thing you'll ever do. Turn the ignition."

Gayle's car fires right up. So far so good. This is one of those cheap manual cars—like Artie's—so Gayle starts giving me all these instructions, such as push this in and let this out and shift this here. I figure how hard can this be, especially if Artie—a person who thinks Beverly Hills is the capital of a state named L.A.—can drive one.

I pull the car away from the curb. The car dies. I give Gayle a pathetic smile.

She nods to indicate "go again."

I get started up again, and this time we actually go down the streets. But it's rather like riding a bucking bull, spurting and jerking. Gayle is shifting back and forth in her seat a lot more than I think is really necessary. She certainly weighs much less than me, and she's bouncing back and forth as if her head is about to go through the windshield. She fastens her seatbelt.

"Look out," she says, grabbing the wheel. Although we are nowhere near it, a beat up old hog blows its horn loud and long. Our car dies and Gayle starts laughing.

"If you laugh at me," I say, "I'm getting out right here and walking."

She keeps laughing, so I open the door to get out.

"Get back here," she says. "I'm not laughing at you. I'm remembering my first time. Relax. And, please, look where you're going."

It gets better pretty fast.

A couple weeks later, after we have driven up and down all the short streets of the park, taking special care to avoid any place Sam might be, Gayle decides that I'm good enough to try a big street. As brave as anything, I start the car and drive up by the store to pick up Colerain Road. I pull out onto the wide four-laner and start to drive down to the 7-Eleven.

It's pretty awful. I mean, you've got all this stuff—turn signals, mirrors everywhere, people on all sides. I don't even notice the usual clutter along the way: the useless iron and brick gates announcing the fancy subdivisions, the thrown-up homely block of stores that last week used to be woods. I don't see any of it. I'm busy hanging-on, hoping I don't get us killed. Gayle tries to help, but she's too busy clutching the sides of the bucket seat. I bet her eyes are closed too.

When I pull into the 7-Eleven lot I am shaking and covered with sweat. I let out the breath I've been holding, turn off the ignition and say, "There."

"Are you getting something here?" Gayle asks.

"I was gonna let you drive back."

She says "no."

"I don't think I can do anymore today. That wore me out."

"I think you better," she says.

I ask her why.

"Because you're scared. And because if you give up on stuff when you're scared, sometimes you give up on it for good."

Though I am ashamed to be doing it, I am trembling and breathing too hard, and even trying not to cry. All the while I know that this driving stuff isn't even that hard.

"I'll wreck your car," I say.

Gayle puts her hand on my shoulder. "You calm down, Marshall. Right now. You take some deep breaths."

I do that.

"Start the car and go," she says. "Now."

I do that.

All the way back to the Park I can feel the muscles in my arm and legs forming knots. Though it's warm, I am shivering. Gayle keeps her hand on my shoulder the whole time, gently whispering instructions. Somehow we make it back to the crackerbox.

"Feels good, doesn't it. You're glad I made you do it, right?"

I agree.

"Let's do one more thing. Let's do a backup. You'll have to do one on the test. Might as well practice everything."

I back up the car up and knock over old man Darcy's trash cans.

"You're supposed to look over your shoulder," Gayle says.

*

Back in the crackerbox Gayle decides that all the hard work deserves refreshment. She pours two tall glasses of iced tea. She's got us drinking it without sugar these days, which isn't so bad. Still, you wouldn't want to do it all the time, and I usually sneak a couple of spoonfuls when she's not looking.

"I guess our man Todd really thinks he's going to save the world," she says.

I tell Gayle that I don't know what to think about Todd these days. "Todd's always been serious about everything: his baseball phase, watching TV, eating. All he does now is think about saving the world. He talks like if you don't actually do something, you're worthless."

I ask Gayle what does she think about that.

"You're asking the wrong person," she says. "You know my militant days are long in the past."

"So you don't think a person has to prove they really care?"

"Care about what, Marshall? Bombs? Some Central American peasants? Why, if they could drop all those bombs on Washington Park and get rid of us—and get away with it—don't think they wouldn't. They'd just as soon be shooting black folks in Saint Louis as communists in Nicaragua."

"So you just do nothing."

"Today I patched up six or seven young men cut up because of drugs. A sister came in to me with two tiny babies. Said the babies were hungry, and that they had no place to go. Couldn't we please get some food for her children.

"That was just part of one day and I go to this job every damn day.

Somedays I come home and am unable to move. Marshall, I don't need to justify myself to some armchair radicals."

Gayle gets up and goes to Sam's room. She says she wants to lie down for a while. I lay myself down on the green plaid sofa. I remember back to April, to lying on the football field: the air-raid siren, the bright sun, the poisoned train.

Did I feel foolish because I lay there just for show, pretending to be dead, or did I feel foolish because Marshall Finney belonged someplace else, taking care of some other business of his own? And how is one to find out what that other business is?

Maybe I just felt foolish.

Gayle says Todd means well.

Always.

She says people like Todd are always thinking, says that Todd has probably been slapped around since birth and that thinking about some nuclear war is better anyway than thinking about what goes on at home.

"So, what should I do?" I ask her later. "What kind of action should I take?"

"My advice, little brother, is to stick with home. Right here. You can never go wrong at home."

That sounds like a good piece of advice to me. I decide to make that Todd's philosophy, too.

*

Sam has been strutting around as if he owned the world. The big shots are up at the dump regularly – the bankers, commissioners, the environmental people. Sam carries his clipboard around and takes them on the tour. He's got this slick black lawyer Gayle found for him guiding the way. Dude's up there whispering in Sam's ear, taking notes. Sam knows just what he wants. He's just not saying yet. And, still, when he wears his overalls, he looks as simple as ever.

The landfill is all covered over with black dirt, all except for a little notch by the Dorset entrance, right where the shed sits. Sam still receives some clean fill along with the shipments of dirt. He's gonna leave that notch for a while. Tax day starts the day the last truck load of dirt comes in. So Slick says.

Most of the old quarry has already sprouted – grass, weeds, wildflowers. The scavenger birds have moved on. Sometimes you see Sam standing up there in the middle of that big field. He just stands up on that hill, grinning, turning in a slow circle.

I watch him from the gate, and when he turns he doesn't see me at all. He spreads his arms like propellers. He is turning and turning. He's turning, the ground spinning under his feet. Who knows what is churning around down in that pit. Something gooey and evil, something that will seep out and get us all. Do you care, Sam? What goes on in your head? What you thinking about up there, anyway?

Sam doesn't care. Not a bit. He spins, he's up there spinning some more.

I expect one day he will take off and fly.

He comes with us on the day of Todd's emancipation hearing. He has his lawyer, Slick, look into the details. Slick says that it's a good idea to have an adult present. He also says the hearing is Todd's show. The judge will talk mostly to him.

Sam looks so sharp this day. He's wearing a real tough-looking sports coat — a dark gray one. He almost looks like one of those slick Clayton lawyers himself.

Slick is right about the hearing. Social workers have done all the work. Todd's parents have been invited to attend the hearing, but they don't show up.

A court appointed guardian does most of the talking for Todd. She reads from the social worker's report. There's nothing new on those pages. Using a lot of fancy language they say that Todd's parents beat him up, threw him out, and don't want him back.

The judge asks Todd if the guardian has fully explained the process. "You are aware of the implications of being emancipated from your parents?"

"Yes, sir."

"Your plans?"

"I'll finish at Eisenhower next year. Then I'll go to college."

The judge nods in approval. All of this is on the papers. There are about an inch of them. Todd's written some. The social workers. Probably Ohairy, too.

"Mr. Finney," the judge addresses Sam.

Sam likes that "Mr. Finney" business, I can tell. His chest puffs up just a bit. "The minor child will be living in your home after emancipation. You've agreed to this? And you understand there will be no support unless provided by the parents?"

"The arrangement is already in place, your honor," Sam says. I bet he said it just the way that Slick told him to. It causes the judge to give Sam a strange look.

The judge congratulates Todd. "You're a lucky young man. Don't blow this chance. Any trouble at school or with the law and we'll have to reexamine this placement."

"You'd send me home?" Todd asks. "Cause I'm not going."

There's a silence while we wait for the judge's response to Todd's boldness.

"Just watch your step," he says calmly. He smiles when he pats Todd on the back.

Then the judge praises Sam some more for taking Todd in. That, of course, puffs his chest out even further.

Sam takes us to Steak 'n' Shake for the celebration lunch. We can have anything we want he says. We eat like pigs.

We pull the truck into the drive and Sam sends me into the cracker-box. He tells Todd to wait just a minute.

A while later they come in. I ask them what they were talking about out there.

They look at each other.

"Mind your own business, why don't you," Todd says.

He and Sam laugh, so I bet it was something good.

I'll bet Sam sat there for a minute with his hands running around the steering wheel, fishing for words. I'll bet Todd sat there looking at his knees.

Sam said something like, "I won't try to take the place of them people down there. They'll always be your folks."

Maybe Todd nodded and maybe Sam told him, "This is your home now. I got my rules and my ways, but I imagine we'll get along pretty good."

Probably Todd was crying by then. Sam handed him the handkerchief from his sports coat, giving maybe a little laugh and telling him to go right ahead.

"Everything's gonna be all right from here on out. Welcome home."

I bet that's just what Sam said.

Later, after Sam has gone up to the landfill, Todd's in the room reading and I'm on the couch watching videos. I hear a bumping outside the door. I peek out of the draperies to see what it is. A hedge by the front door blocks the view, so at first I don't see anything. Then I see a woman walking up the street — a white woman. When I recognize her, I realize it is Todd's mother. She looks back every so often on her way down to the depot and back across the tracks.

I open the door and there is a cardboard box on the porch. I reach down to root around in the box, on top of which is folded something that is gray and striped. I stop rooting when I see the note. Written on a sheet of notebook paper, it says, "FOR TODD."

I carry the box into my bedroom.

"This got left for you," I say. I sit the box down by the rollaway and stand there for a minute with my arms crossed to see what's inside. Todd ignores me and the box, though later when I come get Todd for supper he's wearing a brand-new striped vest.

*

In the mailbox that day is this letter from Rose:

My dear Marshall,

Still no change. Everyday life is the same here. I feel like I've gone around the board only to wind up back at go. So I roll again.

Well, bless her heart, Lucille couldn't wait to tell me about Marshall Field Finney, the new TV star. She means well. Always has.

Oh, to have seen that. You! Up on the TV! Were you scared? Did you show em your stuff?

Lucille expected I'd fall over dead at the news. A few years ago, maybe. Not anymore.

You're your own person now. I told you that before.

Lucille said something about some woman Sam's got. Again expecting me to drop over. I had to smile out here in this desert.

That daddy of yours is something else. You know that, don't you.
Sam, the man.

Dear, sweet Sam. My man.

I want him to be happy. When you love somebody that's what you want for them. Don't know if I want him to be quite that happy. The man is a catch, if you know what I mean. Yes, sir.

You wouldn't know what I was talking about.

Still, I give him my best. Couldn't of done that a year ago either.

When you are alone, you find your strength, Marshall. Your power. Part of mine's knowing Sam will always be right there. Some woman or no.

You'll have that power over people, too. That power to hold on come what may. The power to make people believe that, no matter what else comes along, there will never be anyone like you. I will that power to you. Like me, you will always be loved. Use your powers wisely. Enjoy yourself.

You'll be quite a catch yourself.

The Nevada sun has dried me to a husk. I am fixed to be blown away. I could land almost anywhere. I'm gone.

Forgive me if you want to. I wish you only the best. No more am I a lost and wandering thing.

I choose where I land.

We are linked tighter than fine gold chains. Who knows when we'll next be together. Expect it to be special.

Rose

*

I crumple the letter. Then I straighten it to read it again. I think of Rose out in the desert spring, cherishing her supposed lock on Sam's heart. A pathetic fantasy, that is. One that fills me with pity and sadness. Let her come back and find the truth. We got us a new family here. Me and Sam and Gayle and Todd. I smooth the letter and fold it in with the others. I decide to put her as far from my mind as I can. She is banished. Though the encyclopedia gapes open, I smash it back in there where it belongs, with the rest of them.

*

If I can help it Todd's not going to get into Ohairy's office alone. That is my late spring New Year's Resolution. I have to be real careful, too, because this Ohairy is a crafty one. Todd says that Blondie took him to a meeting of "a new people's coalition of adults advocating change." I tell Todd that it is a shame that none of these "peoples" can speak English and have to resort to words like "coalition" and "movement." That it would probably be better to call themselves a couple of pissed-off guys who want to blow up some buildings.

Todd says that maybe I won't take him seriously but Miss O'Hare will.

Not without me there to keep an eye on her, she won't. We go to her office during a Tuesday study hall. Ohairy congratulates Todd on his newfound freedom. "If there's anything I can do to help you, you be sure and let me know."

"My dad and I are taking care of him just fine," I say to her. I sit down right between the two of them.

"I'm sure you are," she says. She says it with a real fakey smile. She's acting like I'm in her way or something.

Todd can't hardly wait to get started. He rubs his hands together and says, "Wait till I tell you about this meeting." He goes on to tell her how Blondie and he went down to the "people's coalition for big shit," lodge or whatever they call it. He makes a whole performance out of it. He leans forward into her, his elbows rides his knees. He makes choppy little gestures with his hand in Ohairy's direction. Now and then he brushes his hair behind his ears. When he gets to the so-called high points, Ohairy inhales and expands and her little tits pop right up. As he talks he leans closer and she moves closer, too. Her eyes glow like lightning bugs when he talks.

"Mark tells me they're an ambitious group," she says. "You're lucky to get in on the ground floor. You have more say that way. I know I plan to do what I can." She pats him on the back, leaves her hand on his arm. They have to lean around me to do all this. The narrow office seems suddenly narrower, seems to hem us in.

"It makes me kind of nervous," Todd says. "Some of these guys want to do some really radical stuff."

Ohairy shakes her head and says not to worry about it. "Look at the lunch counter sit-ins. Look at the voting rights marches in Alabama. Sometimes you have to do radical things to get results. Sometimes people get hurt."

"That's not necessarily true," I say, before I know what I'm saying. "You could work with people. At a hospital or at a school."

"Marshall! Of course you're right," she says. She says it as if she'd forgotten I was even in the room. "That's what the Peace Corps is all about. I think you'd enjoy something like that. You're a one-to-one kind of guy. You're a people person." She says this with a lot of fake enthusiasm, with a warm smile that leaves me cold. She goes back to Todd.

"There's work for people like us here at home. Right Todd?" They exchange smiles, but they look more like sneers to me.

*

"You don't like Kathy much, do you," Todd says to me. This is later on, at home, after bedtime. With Gayle here, we even have bedtime again.

"Duh," I say.

"I never met anyone like her before," he says. "She's smart. She's got guts. She's not afraid to take charge."

"She jerks people around," I say. "She plays head games."

"Ah, come on. She just wants us to grow. She wants us to get involved with real life."

"Sure," I say. "She wants suckers who are willing to do her dirty work for her."

"Well," Todd says. "I guess that's me, then." He rolls over on the bed. His magazine dumps off the bed as he turns. He has sort of a sickly smile on his face. "Know why I go along with her. I admire her."

"Huh. You're stuck on her."

"Yeah, I guess I'm that, too. You got some heroes, don't you, Marshall?"

"None that I know of. You got to be careful with that stuff. It's easy to get screwed."

"I felt that way. Before I met Kathy. All I knew of life was pot-bellied, beer-guzzling white trash river rats."

"Thanks a lot," I say.

He throws a sock at me. "You know what I mean. People like me: we're on a dead end. That's what Kathy did for me. She showed me a way out. She showed me possibilities."

"There's something sort of . . . slimy about that woman. Hey! You know what we need to do? We need to find you another role model. How about a musician. Or a movie star?"

"I don't know any rockers or any movie stars. I'm happy with what I got. You don't like her because she's different from other teachers. She respects me, and that drives you crazy."

" ' nd it don't hurt that you think she's fine."

"Hey," he says. "I told you a year ago I thought she was hot. Unlike you I'm not ashamed to admit my feelings. I like her. I like her a lot."

"Oh yeah," I say.

Another great comeback.

"Well, I got somebody I'm thinking about, too," I tell him. "I just don't need all of Washington Park to know about it. And I don't need to join some Red-Army-blow-up-the-world club to prove it."

"Kathy had nothing to do with that. I joined that group cause I wanted to."

"You wouldn't know anything about that group if it hadn't been for her."

"And I thank her for that. Kathy and Mark opened my eyes. About a lot of things. You know, Marshall, the world's a lot bigger than what goes on down here in this hollow. You got to get out there into it."

"Why don't you subscribe to *National Geographic,* or something? Give the rest of us a break."

"You're a cynical bastard. If you say one more word, Marshall, I'm picking up your dirty underwear and smothering you with it."

"Just one more thing," I say. "Do you think Randall is sticking it to Ohairy. I mean, I saw them getting down in her office . . ."

I jump off the bed and grab the underwear before Todd can find his glasses. He's saying I'm just like somebody's fuckin old grandma.

"They been living together since college," he yells.

But before he can finish I'm on top of him smothering him with the stretched out pair of Hanes underwear.

I got him pinned. He can't move. I'm so much stronger than he is.

"Say 'I'm a little red-headed commie,'" I taunt.

"Get off of me you big fuckin moose."

"You have to say it," I say.

Just then Sam pounds on the wall. "Cut out all that damn noise in there."

We both jump back in our beds and under the covers. As if that would fool anybody.

"See what you did," I say.

"You're an asshole, Marshall."

"Takes one to know one," I say.

"Don't make me have to come in there," Sam yells.

That's all either of us needs to hear. We're both under the covers and we're both giggling.

*

I wake up that night for my usual 2:30 pee. And I hear them. For the first time I hear them. Sam and Gayle.

It is different than with the others. The same squeaking, of course. But, it is in some way less . . . dangerous sounding. I grab on to the bathroom doorknob so as not to lose my way. I get a little weak at the knees when I've been sleeping.

I wonder how it is she lets him do it. I had never thought she might. But they all do. Every last one of them.

Sam must know the secret word.

*

Sam has planned a big celebration picnic for the Sunday before Memorial Day. He says we've got to celebrate double: the landfill, and also Todd joining our family. He frets over every detail—the right chips, enough soda to drown an army. You'd think we were planning the royal wedding.

After we have packed up the picnic baskets and coolers, Gayle orders them loaded into the Toyota and tells us to meet her on the front lawn.

Out front Gayle starts the big announcement with a fanfare. "Ta-ta-ta-ta-ta-da." She does this pretending she's got a little trumpet held up to her lips. "Gentlemen: I present to you Missouri's newest and certainly most nervous driver—Marshall Field Finney."

"Ta-da." I whip my temporary license out of my pocket. Gayle tosses me the keys. Gayle and I worked almost everyday on this goal. I passed with an 84—that parallel parking gets you every time. As if you had to park that way at the mall anyhow.

Gayle says we can teach Todd next.

"I ain't getting in the car with him," Todd says.

Sam gets a look on face—sort of a big spoiled baby look. "I was gonna show you how to drive." He comes over and half-heartedly shakes my hand. He puts his hands on my shoulders and whispers in my ear. "Didn't you think I was gonna teach you, son?" Then he says loud enough for the others to hear, "I was. But you know how busy I get. I was, though."

Gayle pats him on the back. Tells him to chill out. We get in the car and Sam sits right by me in the front seat. He's got to give directions, since he's the only one who knows where we're going.

Poor Sam. When I get a chance to look down I notice that he's doing as much clutching and shifting and braking as I am. I miss a few turns because Sam is so busy helping me drive that he forgets to tell me where to go.

We drive a long way down Lindberg. Just past the Venture store we make a right turn. We pass a sign that says Laumeier Park. I park the car, and we take the picnic things and follow Sam.

"Look at this place," Sam says. He lets out a big belly laugh. In front of us, all around us in a field, are sculptures — giant pieces of metal, welded, bolted, stacked against each other. Silver, fire red, rusted.

"What is this place?" I ask.

"A park," Sam says. "Let's go."

Sam walks us over by a large orange piece that looks like overgrown bird's wings. We unfold a couple of blankets and use the picnic stuff to stake it out. Then, as if called, we wander away in separate directions to circle the sculptures and gawk. Todd and Gayle circle a wooden thing that is made with old railroad ties.

I find myself standing in front of large rusted girders that are lying against each other as if by accident. I don't know why, but there's something familiar about it, almost friendly. I reach out to touch it.

"Watch your step there, boy." Sam says. He says this coming up behind me. I jump about fifty feet.

Sam lays down on a girder that's angled like a steep red ladder.

"Are you supposed to do that?" I ask him.

"Why not? Why in the hell not? Look at this thing. What do you think it is?"

I shrug. "I don't know nothing about art," I say.

"Yeah, yeah, yeah," Sam says. "I'm just an ignorant old colored man myself, but let me tell you what I think. This here looks to me like some giant dropped a stack of toothpicks and just let em fall where they might."

"How did you find this place anyway?" I ask him.

"It was back a while after Rose left. Sometimes I'd drive around all day. Nothing else to do. I found myself here one day. Kinda by accident, I guess. I kept coming back. Sitting. Walking around.

"Look at that blue piece up yonder. It looks different from here than it looks from over there. You could spend forever looking around in here. Figuring it out."

I say to Sam, "This is a weird place if you ask me."

"But look at all this, Marshall. Why is it all my life nobody told me there could be a place like this? I found it by myself, but it was like it was here waiting for me all along. I think I see things different now than I used to. Look around, son. Tell me what you see."

"I don't think I can do that," I say.

Sam shrugs. He lies back on the girder.

"That's quite all right," he says. "You just think about it." While Sam lies there, I go over and do pullups on a parallel girder.

In a while, Sam sits up.

"Say," he says. He says it a bit too casual I think.

"What's your mama got to say. You know. In them letters she sent you." He doesn't look at me when he says it.

"I only got a couple." I don't look at him either.

I hear him adjust himself. "What she say?"

"Not much. This and that. You know."

Across the way, Todd and Gayle wander around the garden.

"How she doing?"

I shrug.

"How you *think* she doing?"

"Look, I don't know, all right?"

Sam harrumphs.

I turn and face him. "She sounded . . . I don't know. She sounded like herself. You know how she is."

Sam pats the girder, inviting me to sit by him.

I do.

"Yeah, I guess I do know how she is. Where'd you hear from her last? Vegas, right?"

I nod.

"Yeah, boy. She been wanting to get out there a long time. A long time. Think she's okay out there?"

I shrug. "I really don't care," I say.

"Oh, now, Marshall, man. That's your mama there we're talking about."

"She didn't seem too worried about us when she went running off."

Sam rubs his chin. "You still angry, huh."

"What's the big deal all the sudden? I put her out of my mind. Why are you getting into this?"

"You got all the answers, don't you boy." Sam gets up and strolls around the girders. "Well, I been thinking myself lately."

"We're doing pretty good, aren't we?"

"Yeah, we're doing fine. Me and you. But we got us a loose end out there."

"Forget her."

Sam stands behind me with his hands on my shoulders. Kneading them. "You're too hard, son. You got to let go of that anger. It's gonna hurt you. She didn't mean you no harm. That's just not how it was."

"What about you?"

"Me? Look at me. I'm doing fine, aren't I?"

But for a while there . . .

"I ain't got no complaints. Life is pretty good. For me." Sam leans into me with his weight. "What about her? I worry about her. I can't help it. I known her too long."

"Huh?"

"I want to know—what's she doing out there? What's she thinking about? You get all kinds of ideas in your head." He looks off into space.

"What about us? What about what we got here and now?"

Sam spins around almost like that girl in the Sound of Music movie. He looks clumsy and awkward. "This here is a beautiful day."

"I like things just the way they are."

"Well good for you," he says. "Let me see that license."

I unfold it from my pocket and hand it to him. Sam reads it and taps it against his hand.

"I was planning to show you how to drive. I was looking forward to it." He hands back the paper. I fold it up slowly and put it away.

"You're getting to be a man now. Just look at you." He grabs my face and rubs his hands over my chin. "You been shaving?"

"No, sir."

"Pretty soon. Pretty soon." He goes behind me and grabs a handful of hair. "You and me, we in this together now. From now on. I won't let you down. Never again. I'm gonna show you, son. Show you how a man does. You with me?"

I nod my head.

"It's a lot of things, being a man. It's the way you do folks, and how you handle yourself. It's how you treat the women and it's your word of honor. I'm teaching you everything I know. I was gonna start with the driving, but we can go on from there."

He lets out a sigh. "Oh, I know old Gayle meant well. She's a good old girl. But me, I was gonna show you the right way. You know I love em, but women don't drive worth a shit. I'm proud of you, though. My boy got him a license." Sam slaps me on the shoulder. A little too hard, I think.

"You gonna get me a car?"

He laughs long and hard, his loud laugh filling the whole park.

*

Later under the orange wings we feast on crispy fried chicken, bread and butter sandwiches and fresh strawberries. The May sun stands high overhead in a clear blue sky. I reach over to flip on the box.

"No. Listen," Sam says.

The air is full of the soft sound of birds, almost trembling with their sweet music. A spring breeze sweeps around the sculptures, whispering as it passes.

Sam inhales deeply, taking in as much of the air as he can. Sometimes he seems like such a silly man. Worrying after people who don't give a damn about him. At those times, if you took a knife to him you could cut through that onion skin and peel it away in a flash. Sam, the sap, but don't you be fooled. He is not really that way at all. He is awesome. For nothing he could wrap his big hands around your neck and strangle the life out of you. You get on with Sam the way you get on with a pet tiger—on his terms. Sam lets out that air with a roar.

He rises at his place and orders us all to stand with him. "A toast to you all: Big things are coming—really big things. I hope, for you, Marshall, for all of us, that all our days are as happy as this one."

We raise our glasses to Sam.

Still, later we lie separate on our backs, scattered like the rusted girders of the sculpture—yet just like them we are connected. It is a family sculpture, see. Each piece holds up another, and you can't imagine what would happen should you remove any part. Though we are not touching I am aware of each one: Sam, his head near mine, Gayle just next to him, Todd, his arm parallel to my own. We lie in peace. The sun, crossing over to evening, warms us to the core.

16

 It's AS IF Todd's been electrified the whole week before Memorial Day. You tap him on the shoulder, he's startled. The phone rings, he jumps.

"You've got to tell me what's up," I say.

Finally, on Thursday, he cracks. "You have to swear you won't tell your dad. Or anyone."

I hate it when people say that: You know it means trouble. Still, I do. I swear.

"I've been telling you something big was being planned. Saturday's the day."

I can't myself believe these people are going to ruin a perfectly good holiday weekend with some demonstration. Still, I keep my mouth shut. I ask for the details.

"You've heard of Aaron Young, the peace activist. He's been sentenced to two years for breaking into the Calhoun Nuclear Reactor site."

"So you guys have decided to break in and go to jail with him."

"We're chaining ourselves to the fence of the Old Courthouse. We're staying until he's released."

"Does this mean you won't be having barbecue on Monday?" Sam always barbecues on Memorial Day — makes a big production out of it, invites the whole family and everyone else in Washington Park, too.

"I'm kinda scared," Todd says. He gets up and starts pacing. "Mark says there could be trouble. Serious trouble. He says someone tipped off the cops."

"I think they usually show up at this kinda thing anyway," I say.

"Mark says that they have no intention of allowing any demonstration at all. He says to expect a confrontation. People may get hurt."

"So don't go," I say.

"I have to do this," Todd says.

"Why?"

"Because. For me. I don't want people to think I . . ."

"Who cares what people think."

"My effort . . ." Todd starts. He pauses and paces, just as if he were on the edge of figuring something out. "I can make a difference at this demonstration. I believe that. This my big chance. I have to do it. For me."

Though this may be the only opportunity to get my two cents in, I resist. Todd is so serious just now, it somehow doesn't seem right.

I say to him, "You gotta do what you gotta do."

"I need for you to go with me, Marshall. Please."

I shake my head to indicate I'm not sure.

"I don't expect you to join the protest. Not unless you really want to, that is."

"I'll pass."

"Just be around in case anything happens, okay?"

I tell him "Sure." Then we go up to Miss Ida's to ask Artie to drive us down there. Sam's not about to loan me his truck — at least not until I'm shown "the right way to drive."

We decide to leave Gayle out of this mess. She hasn't been around in a couple of days anyway. It's just as if she's disappeared. I ask Sam about her, but he just shrugs. He says she's around somewhere, he supposes.

*

The big demo's set for ten A.M. Saturday morning.

At nine Sam and Todd and I are sitting around at breakfast. All of us are acting as dumb as can be. Sam's got on one of his nice sports coats again.

"Nice day," I say.

"Beautiful day," Sam says. He exaggerates the "beautiful."

"Yup, it's gonna be a good day," Todd says. "I can feel it."

This is the general stream of the conversation.

Finally, Sam stands up and announces he's got to meet some men up at the landfill. "Big doins," he says, raising his eyebrows.

As soon as he's out of sight, Todd and I take off running towards Miss Ida's store. "Dammit, we're gonna be late," Todd says.

We go barreling into the store like robbers.

"You boys are in quite a hurry," Miss Ida says.

"We're late," I say. I'm breathing so hard, that's all I can say.

"I hope you all are not in a big rush. I don't even know if Baby Boy is up yet. Let me call him." She goes to the bottom of the steps.

"Arthur," she yells.

Todd is practically coming out of his skin. He's pacing around, pounding his fist into his hand.

Miss Ida is giving him the eye. She's suspicious, I can tell.

At last, here comes old Artie ambling down the steps like he owns the store. He's wearing his red and black breakdance outfit. It includes red sunglasses.

"Jesus," mumbles Todd.

"Where's my breakfast?" Artie whines. He's got the nerve to be cranky and belligerent, too.

"I had breakfast out at eight o'clock," Miss Ida shouts. "If you can't get your lazy black butt out of bed, it's not my problem." She looks over to Todd and me and points her thumb at the door. "Get this simple boy out of my face."

Artie stomps out, grabbing a Hostess cupcake on the way. We wave at Miss Ida.

"Keep him," she hollers.

"All right, let's move it," Todd says. We tumble into Dentyne. Artie just sits there behind the wheel.

"I don't have any gas," he says.

"We'll stop at Vicker's and get some. Get moving," Todd orders. He's pounding on the top of the seat.

"I don't have any extra money," Artie says. "I got a date tonight with Susan."

Todd and I look at each other. Todd's about to strangle him.

"Drive down to my house," I say. "I'll run in and get some."

Todd sits back and stews.

*

When we pull up in front of the crackerbox, Gayle's Toyota is parked out front. I run inside and find her loading up stuff into a box and a suitcase.

"Marshall," she says as if I had scared her. "I didn't expect to see you."

"What are you doing?" I ask her.

"Don't you and the fellas usually go to the mall Saturday morning? I um . . ." She trails off. The handful of stuff she carries – sweaters, towels, blouses – hangs limp in her arms.

"Where are you going?"

She sits down in the recliner. "I'm a coward," she says. "Maybe that's the big difference between me and your mother."

A loud honk comes from Dentyne.

"Did you and Sam have a fight?"

"I wish. I wish we'd had the biggest fight since Ali-Frazier." She gets up. Says, "This isn't good." She takes a box to the kitchen to pack up her wheat germs, her herbal teas, her french mustards.

"Just like that. You up and leave just like that. Without saying good-bye or drop dead or . . ."

The horn honks loud and long.

"Your friends are waiting for you," Gayle says. Cold and cool.

I run over to the screen door and wave at them. I yell, "I'm coming, just hold on."

"Where is Sam? Does Sam know what's going on here?"

"I don't report to Sam Finney."

The horn again. I go yell again. Todd's standing outside the car with his arms crossed, red in the face – redder than I've ever seen him. I stick up five fingers, mouth "five minutes."

"I think I deserve an explanation," I say to Gayle.

"You don't deserve nothing from me, boy." She says this angry. A hard look sets on her face.

I go back to my room to get the money. I have no idea where to look for it. I open drawers, slam stuff around. I can't think, can hardly breathe. My eyes are full of water.

Gayle puts her hands on my shoulders. "I'm sorry," she says. She sits me down on my bed with her arm around me. There is the continuous drone of the horn. Mostly in my head.

"What I'm doing is hard enough," she says. "This part, the part with you, Marshall: I knew I wasn't strong enough to do this."

I ask her what it is she has to do.

"When I hooked up with y'all, I knew it might only be for a short while. I figured it might be worth a trip."

She gets up and wanders around the room. "It has been, too — quite a trip indeed. This has been one of the best times in my whole life."

I wipe away with my hand at the tears which I'm trying to control. "You don't have to go," I whisper.

Like a ghost she already is fading. "This isn't my home. You know I can't stay here, Marshall."

"We were a family. A happy one."

"Not your *real* family, Marshall." Her voice sounds distant. A horn honks loudly.

"Your friends are waiting." Gayle pulls me up from the bed and walks me through the house to the front door. She wipes at my eyes with a Kleenex. She's picked up the crumpled ten dollar bill I've dropped. Mashing it into my hand, she plants a kiss on my cheek.

"Wait, please. Wait till I come back," I say.

I see her smiling in the door.

Waving goodbye.

*

It's nine forty-five. Todd is practically in pieces from nerves.

"Stop at the dump," I order.

Artie whines, but I yell at him. "Just do it."

Todd hits the back seat with his hand, cursing under his breath.

"Thirty seconds," I beg. "Okay? A minute at the most."

"Marshall, I promised I'd be at the Courthouse when they started. People are counting on me."

"Then leave me. I've got to talk to Sam."

I jump out before the car stops and run toward Sam. He's standing on the hill with a couple of dudes wearing black suits. One of them is the lawyer, Slick.

Dentyne doesn't move. I guess they decided to wait.

Sam's probably in the middle of another story. About mafia cars. About little boys stuck in piles of silt. His audience is in his thrall.

"Can I talk to you, daddy?"

"In a minute, son. We're about done with our business." Sam has a clipboard full of papers. One of the suits indicates to the other one two points on the horizon.

"I need to talk to you now," I say.

Sam points me up to the shed. "Wait for me back there," he says to me. As if I was another one of his flunkies.

I give him a look meaner than one of his own.

I walk back to the car and tell Artie to get me the hell out of here. He does.

*

Artie stops the car in a space on Chestnut at the corner of Broadway. The three of us get out and lean on Dentyne's rusty rump.

"There they are," I say.

Todd doesn't say anything. Now that we've rushed halfway across North America, he's not so eager.

The demonstrators — Todd's good buddies — are gathered on the steps of the Old Courthouse. There are only about thirty or so. They are in something of a huddle. From here, it looks like they are praying. I spot Blondie in the center of the crowd. Around him I see some of Todd's recruits from Eisenhower. They look young, eager, and scared.

A small group of supporters stands on the walkway with signs saying things like "Free Aaron Young" and "Justice Must Be Served." They sing "We Shall Not Be Moved" in loud, earnest voices. In that little group is Miss O'Hare.

"This is an illegal gathering," calls a policeman through his bullhorn. "Clear the area at once." A company of his men stands in a line at the fence, helmeted and at attention.

"Pretty intense," I say.

Artie wants to know where the TV cameras are. Todd just stands there. Swallowing. Fidgeting.

A group of three from the steps comes to the fence. Cheers of encouragement fill the air. As they attempt to handcuff and chain themselves to the wrought iron, two or three officers get on each one and pull them away. There is a fight. Three fights. The demonstrators are dragged away kicking and screaming. The officers stay cool, but defend themselves. They drag the men and women away. It takes two or three of them to carry the hands and feet.

The next three go to the fence.

"I didn't expect anything like this," Todd says. He's rubbing his hands together, rubbing them on his jeans.

"Police brutality," chants Ohairy's group.

"This area will be cleared," the officer announces.

One of the women screams loudly. Somehow she's been kicked in the head. We can see all of this. Todd flinches. His whole body tenses.

"I don't know about this," he says. "What should I do, Marshall?"

Three by three the demonstrators attempt the fence. Just that way they are stopped, they fight, and are hauled away. The young recruits fight wildly. They curl up quick and tight like centipedes.

Artie wants to go home. He is afraid of trouble from Miss Ida.

I am riveted. It feels strange to be so excited. Here is something happening that you could be a part of. Here are some people making something happen. Putting it on the line. For just a minute I am ready to go over there myself.

Then Artie whines my name. I see a woman tossed into the back of the police van like a sack of potatoes. Ouch. I reach for the door.

Just as Artie is fishing for his keys, Blondie sees Todd and then Ohairy does, too. They beckon him with their hands. They are calling him over as if to a party, calling him to join the fun.

Todd straightens his back. He slowly makes ready to go.

"Wish me luck," he says.

He's going. I can't believe he's found the courage to go.

From somewhere it comes over me. Some sort of resolve, some way of deciding things.

"No," I say.

I grab Todd's arm. Tight. First one hand on one arm, then the other on his other. I hold him from behind.

With their hands Ohairy and Blondie call. Insisting.

"Let me go," he says. He's pulling against me. "I'm going. I'm going with them."

I tell Artie to get in the car.

"You're staying with us," I tell Todd.

He struggles. He reaches the peak of his determination.

But I am as strong as I've ever been. Maybe as strong as Sam himself. Across the way it continues: the chanting, the charging, the fighting, some blood. Ohairy faces us now — her arms crossed. She's willing me to free Todd.

"I mean it, Marshall. You let me go.'"

I hold on tight. And even though I can feel him weakening, know he's running out of courage, know I've won, even as they haul away the last of the demonstrators, I hold on. I'm still holding on as we watch them go. Holding on even though Todd has collapsed against me. Defeated. As if someone's let all the air out of him.

"Sometimes I hate you, Marshall," he says.

I tell him that that's okay.

And there we are. Artie leaning against the window on his hands. Todd leaning on me. Collapsed. Me holding on to him.

Holding on still as if our lives depended on it.

*

Artie drives us home. I sit in the back with Todd. I don't care how it looks. He is still collapsed against me.

"Do you want a hamburger?" I ask.

"Let's just go home," he says.

Later he asks, "Do you think they'll hate me?"

Here is what Artie says. Real proud, he says this. Just like it was a sermon. He says:

"It doesn't matter what they think. It only matters what we think — your family and friends. The people who love you."

He says it just like that. Or that's the way I write it down. Such bull, and yet so perfect. I had to write it down.

And it was then I decided, you see. I was going to write it all down, all of this. A person could spend their entire life doing something like that.

I sit up to rub Artie on the head. He may not be smart, but a lot of times he ends up being right. He wears great clothes, too.

Who else would wear a breakdance outfit to a riot?

As I lean up, Todd falls down on the seat behind me, laughing. Laughing like someone on the crazy ward at Malcolm Bliss.

"What's so funny?" I ask.

"Fuck em," he says. "If they can't take a joke, fuck everybody in the whole goddamn world."

*

We stop into Miss Ida's store for some sodas.

Before we can get them, Miss Ida says to me, "Sam said to tell you to hustle your butt on home and to do it quick."

She says it with a big suspicious smile on her face. Sam must have something big on his mind.

"Let's go," I say to Todd.

"I'm going down the hollow for a bit. To see my mom."

"Be careful," I say.

"Don't worry. My dad's always gone this time on Saturdays. Prime drinking time. I'll be home later."

I pat him on the back. He is wearing his new gray-striped vest. He wears that a lot these days.

*

I go running down the hill like I'm flying. Sam's talked Gayle into staying with us.

Forever. I know it.

I can't wait to tell them what we did. And didn't do. I can't wait to tell Gayle what I decided.

"Tell me when you know what you want to do with your life," she'd said. And now I know.

Hang on Washington Park. Your story is safe no more. I'm telling it all.

The town's stories.

Sam's stories.

Stories I make up.

The whole bit.

The dirt that gets done, the rotten things we do to each other, the good times, the parties, how everybody looks out for everybody else.

Must be somebody out there wants to hear all this.

I'm running down that hill like I'm flying, and I can see here comes Sam, coming out to meet me. Come on, come on, he's waving. Waving with his hands. Waving the clipboard full of papers.

I'm running toward Sam like a kid, as fast as I can. His eyes are big, popped out of his head, and his face glowing bright as anything. He is like a kid, too.

"There you are," he says. "We've been waiting for you."

"I'm here," I say, and he reaches out with his hand and grabs my arm.

"She's here," he says. "Everything's gonna be all right."

"Thank God," I say.

If you want anything bad enough you will get it.

"Come on," Sam says, pulling me into the crackerbox. And then, "Where?" He is vibrating with excitement.

She comes in from the hallway.

"There she is," Sam says.

And there she is indeed. The desert sun has baked her medium brown. Her fingernails are still bright red.

"What is this?" I ask.

"Baby," she says.

"See here," Sam says. "Back in one piece. Good as new. Don't she look good." He's got his hand wrapped around my bicep. Like I'm his prisoner. I wrench free.

"What do you want?" I ask. Real quiet. I take a step toward her. "Why didn't anybody tell me? You all don't tell me anything."

She looks down at her shoes. She mumbles something. Something about surprise.

"Boy . . ." Sam threatens.

She raises a hand to still him.

My arm starts shaking where he had me. I hold onto it with the other arm.

"What is this?" I ask again.

"I guess I'm back," she says. "Gonna give the mama thing one more try." She laughs as if that is a joke.

"Back where she belongs," Sam adds.

I shake my head.

"Not fair," I say. It comes out a squeak.

"Boy . . ." Sam growls. His hand pushes my back. The fool is hitting me. Or pushing me toward her.

"You gonna be a man, boy." He orders it. "I told you, and you're gonna start right now."

She raises her head, juts out her chin.

"Marshall and I can work this out," she says. "Can't we, baby?"

"You always ruin things," I say, shaking my head. "Always. It's just . . . not supposed to be this way."

She reaches for me with her red nails.

17

"GET UP," Sam says. "Get up and come with me."

I am lying on my back in my bedroom with my arms folded across my chest. I am staring at the white ceiling. Staring at the gravel. Not going anywhere.

This is what happens when you stick with home.

Staring. I can't get through.

"Come with me, son. I want you right by my side."

Sam's voice is quiet and sweet.

Here I am: come to the end of a story I am unable to finish. If I lie here I can become solid — as hard and as rigid as a stainless steel vault. I will my muscles to freeze. I breathe only to exhale the fire that's burning inside me.

"We come so far. Together. We just got this little bit left to go. We can make it. Come on."

This is how the story goes. I can remember each and every blessed word. I can tell it with precision, with a razor sharp memory. I can make it seem just as if it is happening right now. For what it's worth, because I can't make it end any other way. I can't make it come out with me strong, with me the hero.

I don't look good at the end.

I didn't know enough, you see. Try to understand. This is just the way it was.

"Look at what I have for you."

I don't want to see, yet I do see. Him strolling, sheepishly, across my room. Him laying the paper on my stomach.

"It's for you."

I stare.

He backs away out of the edge of my sight as if he were a dream. I close my eyes to make it all disappear. The stories I don't control. The stories that aren't my stories. I close my eyes to keep away the tears. I push out the walls with everything I've got.

"Took in my last load this week — of trash, dirt, of everything. Forever. That there is your deed and this one is mine. Fifty/fifty. Course we can switch halves. If you want. You can do whatever you want. I might build that roller coaster. Or take a trip to the moon. What are you gonna do, Marshall?"

I'm going to be whole and solid: I'm going to be a slab of carved marble. Not in some silly park. In a museum behind velvet ropes, where no one can touch me. I'm going to lie here on this bed forever and wish away the softening that is already starting at the edges.

"You can't lie there forever, son. You'll try, I bet. But you won't. I'll still be here anyway. When you open your eyes guess whose face you'll see? So come on."

He'll be there forever — not even Houdini could make him disappear.

And they are inside my head anyway — all the Sams: the mean ones, the silly ones, the drunk ones, the silent ones. The ones with skin as thin as an onion. When I open my eyes, which Sam will I see?

I am already as soft as a cotton stuffed toy.

"Look at me."

I turn my head. Open my eyes.

Sam is a tall man, about 6'4". His shoulders are broad, every inch of him is solid, heavy with flesh. His head is large and square with skin the warm brown, almost red color of wet freshly turned earth. Large black glowing eyes. A mouth full of teeth that often smile without meaning to. Enormous feet — Sam has these enormous feet. And hands, huge hands. And . . . And there is Sam: nodding, becoming a watery blur.

"My sweet Rosey. I love her," he shrugs. "You're gonna have to trust me. We — all of us — we gonna live happily ever after. I just love her."

Is that true? Did I know? Would it have made any difference?

Yes.

Because that is a different story altogether.

Instead:

this is how I am to be lost: lying on my back, pretending forever to be only myself. Dissolved, no longer ignoring the huge hands reaching out for me, like a magnet, pulling me to the end, to the end of this story. This story.

If only I'd known.

Instead:

"Come on," Sam says.

"Come."

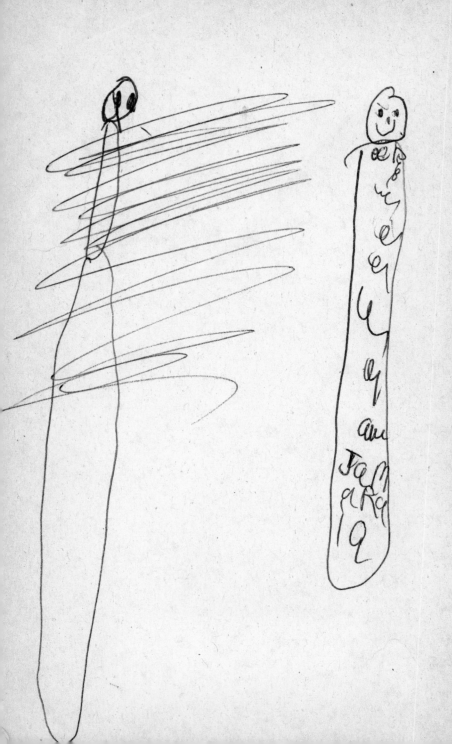

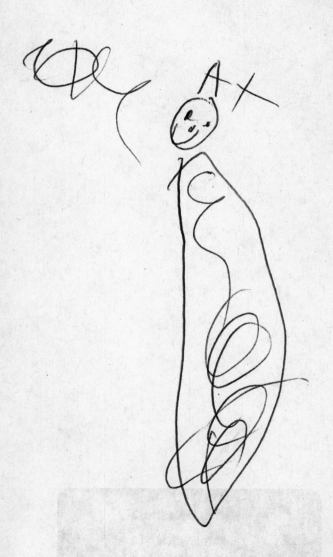